BLOOD BROTHERS

BLOOD BROTHERS

S. A. HARAZIN

DELACORTE PRESS

Published by Delacorte Press
an imprint of Random House Children's Books
a division of Random House, Inc.
New York

Delacorte Press and colophon are registered trademarks of Random House, Inc.

www.randomhouse.com/teens

Educators and librarians, for a variety of teaching tools, visit us at
www.randomhouse.com/teachers

Library of Congress Cataloging-in-Publication Data

Harazin, S. A.
  Blood brothers / S.A. Harazin. — 1st ed.
    p. cm.
  Summary: With his best friend on life-support after taking drugs at
a party, seventeen-year-old Clay, a medical technician, recalls their
long friendship, future plans, and recent disagreement, and tries to
figure out who is responsible for the accidental overdose.
  ISBN: 978-0-385-73364-9 (trade) — ISBN: 978-0-385-90379-0 (glb)
  [1. Medical care—Fiction. 2. Best friends—Fiction. 3. Friendship—
Fiction. 4. Drug abuse—Fiction. 5. Self-esteem—Fiction.
  6. Georgia—Fiction.]   I. Title.
PZ7.H2114Blo 2007
[Fic]—dc22
                                        2006019637

The text of this book is set in 12-point Goudy.
Book design by Cathy Bobak

Printed in the United States of America

10 9 8 7 6 5 4 3 2

First Edition

This is for Patrick, Katie, Andrew,
and Thomas Harazin.

BLOOD BROTHERS

CHAPTER 1

Saturday, 6 PM

I hurry down the cold hospital corridor and barge through the automatic doors of the emergency department. My sneakers squeak on the glossy white tiles I mopped this morning and catch on the hem of my blue scrubs, pulling them below my hips. I glance around, embarrassed, pull up my pants, and tighten the drawstring around the waist. These things never seem to fit me right.

I have a dull headache from the twelve-pack of beer I drank last night as I watched cars pass by on the highway. That's what passes for entertainment here in Georgia. Thankfully, I only threw up once this morning, but I haven't eaten anything all day.

I adjust my stethoscope and my name tag.

CLAY GARDENER. MED TECH I.

This means I do anything I'm told to do. I'm seventeen years old, the youngest employee at the hospital.

I stop at the nurses' station. Empty metal charts litter the desk. Mrs. Hunt, the nursing supervisor, is talking on the two-way radio. Five minutes ago she paged me and asked me to empty the trash in the ER.

"Can you airlift the patient to the nearest trauma center, over?" she's saying.

"Biggs, that's a negative. ETA in three to five minutes. Unit one, over and clear."

Mrs. Hunt glances my way. "Clay, help me set up for a trauma patient."

I swallow, but my mouth is still dried out from last night's beer. I hope I know what to do. "Yes, ma'am," I answer.

The other employees call her Big Mama behind her back. I don't. Well, sometimes, maybe. She hired and trained me for my job here as an orderly. I get to do what nobody else wants to do. I'm the one who mops the vomit or blood off the emergency room floor or wipes sweat from the gurneys. I work all over the hospital. Most people see my job as nothing but menial labor, but Mrs. Hunt says I'm an important part of the team, and she gives me more responsibility than a lot of the other orderlies have. She says I'll make a great doctor one day. Sometimes I imagine myself as a doctor, but then I get a big lump in the back of my throat. I don't like dreaming the impossible.

She's a big lady, and she's good with little kids and drunks. I've heard she deals with little kids and a drunk at home. She loves hearing about the cross-country bike trip my best friend,

Joey, and I plan to take next year and my desire to go to college. But I have to win the lottery first to be able to pay tuition, and then actually get admitted somewhere.

In the trauma room, Mrs. Hunt flips switches and turns dials. Sounds of bubbling, swishing, and beeping fill the air.

I pull yellow plastic gowns, masks with goggles, and gloves from overhead cabinets.

Mrs. Hunt connects clear blue tubing to the oxygen. "You were late again today," she says.

This morning I rode my bike four miles to work with a hangover. I don't plan on ever doing that again.

I place a lift sheet on the gurney. Head down, I smooth out the wrinkles. I imagine the suction machine is draining all the oxygen from the room. I force in a breath. "Yes, ma'am. It won't happen again. I promise."

I glance at my watch. I get off at 7 PM. I've been here almost twelve hours, but it feels like a hundred.

Mrs. Hunt unfolds a blue pad and places it at the head of the stretcher. She doesn't smile or nod. I wonder how mad she is at me for coming in late again. I get the backboard and place it on the gurney.

I hear sirens blasting. The double doors of the ambulance entrance whoosh open and two EMTs slide a stretcher inside as they perform CPR.

"Sixteen-year-old female. Car accident. No seat belt. Went through the windshield," an EMT says. "We arrived within five minutes . . . started CPR."

"Call a code," Mrs. Hunt says. She wiggles into a yellow gown. "Thank God you got her intubated," she tells the EMTs.

I pick up the phone and press a button. "Code blue, emergency room." I say the words three times.

We lift the patient onto the gurney. I cut off her shirt with a pair of scissors, right down the middle. Mrs. Hunt connects the hospital heart monitor. CPR is in progress. I pull the emergency cart and defibrillator next to the patient. Dr. Murphy, Guthrie—a nurse—and a respiratory therapist appear.

"Start a large-bore IV," Dr. Murphy barks. "Give her bicarb followed by one milligram of epi. Check the ET and continue to hyperventilate. Bolus her with two hundred fifty of saline." I'm glad I'm not the one who has to remember all those orders.

The respiratory therapist listens to the girl's chest. "Breath sounds in both fields," she says.

One EMT steps out of the way and starts writing on a metal clipboard. "She was in full cardiac arrest when we arrived on the scene. Pupils already fixed and dilated," he says.

I look at the girl. A breathing tube sticks out of her mouth, held in place by tape. Her face is twilight blue, caked with dried blood.

I hope it isn't too late for you.

I can feel my heart speed up.

I hear the hiss of the oxygen, the gurgling of the suction, the beep of the heart monitor, the sounds of life clinging to this world. The one thing I can't handle is someone dying before my eyes. That's happened a couple of times. In both cases I got an urge to shut all the windows and doors in the room so the patient's soul wouldn't escape, so maybe we could still save them. There aren't any windows in this room, and the door's already shut.

The girl's jeans are ripped at one knee where her leg is partially severed. The respiratory therapist squeezes oxygen into her lungs with the ambu bag. Her chest rises and falls each time. I can smell blood and alcohol.

"Clay!" Mrs. Hunt says, preparing a syringe of medication. She's a big yellow blob calling to me from inside a tunnel. I hear a faint buzz. It's like we're inside a giant refrigerator.

"Clay! Take over compressions."

I put on a face shield and move to the side of the gurney. The other EMT steps out of the way. I position my hands in the right spot and press. This is not the plastic dummy I practiced on when I was getting certified. This is a real person. Not too hard. Press down an inch. Don't break the ribs. I count. I'm shaking, sweating, gasping. A properly trained person can do effective CPR. You don't have to be a doctor. Any CPR is better than none.

"Good femoral pulse with CPR," Guthrie says. I see her wink at me like she's saying I'm doing well.

We all have a role. Dr. Murphy calls out orders. Mrs. Hunt prepares the medication, then hands it to Guthrie, who injects it. The respiratory therapist ventilates the patient. Because no one else is here to do it, I perform compressions.

"Are her parents here?" Dr. Murphy asks Guthrie. He's sticking a needle into the girl's groin to get a blood gas. Dark blood fills the syringe. Dark blood means no oxygen. Bright red blood, good oxygen.

"On the way," Guthrie says. "I've already asked the receptionist to notify the hospital chaplain and organ procurement."

Her words slice into me like a knife. But I keep working, mostly unaware of what's going on around me. Focused. I'm doing the compressions correctly. No one yells and says I can't do anything right, or that I'm an idiot.

Dr. Murphy flashes a light into the patient's eyes. "Fixed and dilated." He shakes his head. "Stop CPR. Let's see what we have." He checks for a femoral pulse.

I stare at the girl. Her tits are blue-black. I gasp. I bet she was pretty before her head smashed into the windshield. A straight line moves slowly across the heart monitor.

"Continue CPR," Dr. Murphy says after a few seconds. "Let's keep trying."

I put the heel of my palm on her chest and start pumping.

"Repeat epi," the doctor says, and Guthrie hands Mrs. Hunt the syringe of medicine that might stimulate the heart.

Warm mist from my breathing clouds my face shield as beads of sweat collect on my forehead. I glance at the girl from the corner of my eye.

I don't want to think of you as a person. Now you're just a broken machine we're trying to fix.

"She's fibrillating," Dr. Murphy says, and I see an erratic line on the monitor. "Defib at two hundred."

Yes! There's a chance to get her back.

Mrs. Hunt places special pads on the chest. Guthrie charges the paddles to 200 and places them on the pads. "Clear," she calls out, and looks around. Everybody steps back. She presses the buttons on the paddles. The electrical shock surges through the girl. Her body springs forward as if instantly brought back to life. The doctor looks at the monitor.

"Still fibrillating," Dr. Murphy says. "Defib at three hundred."

And the same thing happens. With every passing second, her grip on life loosens.

"Three sixty," the doctor says.

She's shocked again, but the erratic line straightens out into asystole. Into nothing.

"Continue CPR," Dr. Murphy says in a voice as flat and thin as the line on the monitor. "Try epi down the ET tube. How long has it been?"

Mrs. Hunt glances at the clock on the wall that doesn't tell time. It shows only how long we've been trying. "Twenty minutes," she answers.

My shoulders sag over the patient as I keep trying to force the beat back into her heart. "Pupils blown," somebody says, and I imagine an explosion inside her head. I look at the girl again.

"Continue," Dr. Murphy says. "Let's give the epi a few seconds to reach the heart."

"But her pupils are blown," Guthrie repeats.

"We're giving it all we've got," Dr. Murphy says.

Don't die, don't die, don't die. Can't you hear me? You can't die when we're doing all we can to save you.

A few more minutes pass. The doctor tells me to stop. "Still no pulse without CPR," Guthrie says finally.

The doctor breathes in deep and lets it out slow. "Let's call it." He removes his gloves, his face mask, his gown. He slams them into the trash. "We can't do anything more." He frowns, and his big brown eyes glisten in the bright light.

I don't want to stop. I want to tell the girl I'm sorry we can't save her, that I'm sorry she's dead and won't ever go to college, or fall in love, or do anything she ever dreamed of doing. I'm sorry she won't ever be able to get mad over something stupid. I'm sorry, but we gave everything we had to give.

"Thank you," Dr. Murphy tells us. "For all your help."

I stand there and listen. All I can hear is a buzz from a machine. All I can see is the dead girl. She fills the room even though she's just a small, still body on the metal table.

"I can't do this right now," Guthrie says. "I'll be back in a few minutes to finish up." I pull the sheet over the girl. I won't leave her lying there naked. On the way out, I leave the door cracked just in case there really is a soul and it needs to escape.

I step into the waiting room in time to hear the wailing of the girl's mother, her father's anguish. Head down, I start thinking about Michelle, about Joey, about myself—and it hits me. What right do I have to be so pissed about how they treated me? Everything that's happened with them seems about as important as bird droppings when a teenage girl dies in front of you.

CHAPTER 2

Saturday, 8:05 PM

I trudge across Joey's backyard to the shed. The sun's setting, and I'm not feeling as down as I was when I left the hospital. In fact, I feel hopeful—like I have some perspective, and me and Joey, and maybe even Michelle—we're all going to be okay. The air smells green from the tomato vines leaning against the side of the building. The vines grew in just a couple of months from the seeds of rotten tomatoes that Joey and I had thrown at each other.

I come here a lot. The shed's always been a second home to me, even though it's just a small, slapped-together building half filled with garden tools.

I push open the door, hoping I don't smell like hospital and death. "Joey, I need to talk to you. I'm sorry about—"

My mouth freezes. I stand still for a minute as my eyes take in the mess. The table in the middle of the room lies on its side, and beer-bottle glass shines on the concrete floor like discarded jewels. The radio on the counter by the sink plays "Let It Be," garbled by static. I smell alcohol and stale smoke instead of the usual grass and dirt. A pile of Joey's clothes lies next to the bunk bed, and he's left his cell phone on the floor.

I whistle. "What the hell happened in here, man?" I shout, turning in all directions, finally fixing my stare on the storage room. We never go in there, but it's weird that the door is completely shut. "Don't you think we're a little old for hide-and-seek, Joey?"

He has to be in the storage room. I chuckle. "Jesus, Joey. What'd you do all day?" For the record, Joey and I are not big partyers. Last night's beer binge was a first for me, and it definitely wasn't a party. I was drinking alone and feeling sorry for myself. But Joey must have had a bunch of people over, to generate this kind of mess. I'm surprised he'd do that—and in the middle of the day. I check my watch—it's only a little after eight, and apparently the party's already over. Unless they're all in on a practical joke.

I set the table upright.

"You got some friends in there with you, Joey?" I call, laughing. "Are we back in third grade? This shit doesn't scare me, guys."

The window curtains above the sink rustle. I go over and look outside. I only see Joey's car in the driveway. He's not anywhere in sight. I pick up the cell phone and dial the house in case he's inside asleep, though he'd be careless to leave the place in this shape. If his parents happened to look in the shed—I don't even want to imagine their reaction.

The phone rings and rings until the voice mail answers like it did when I called before I left the hospital.

I glance at his white T-shirt on the floor. Two red spots stain the front. They could be ketchup or blood. I vote ketchup. The kid is smart, but he's a damn sloppy eater.

I consider just lying outside on the lawn until he gets tired of hiding and comes out to get me. I could use the nap.

Then I hear a thud from the storage room. I grin. I can't help it. He wants me to open the door so he can pounce on me. I'm glad everything's all right with us now.

I walk over to the storage area and open the door. "This is really lame," I say, prepared for him to jump in front of me and scream like an idiot.

A thirty-watt bulb hangs from the ceiling. The dim light reveals Joey hiding, only partly out of sight, next to the tool shelves. He's gripping a hoe. I take a deep breath. It smells like a rat died in here. You wouldn't believe how horrible a rat can smell after a couple of days in a trap.

"Yeah, um, I can see you over there," I say in a deadpan voice. "You've got to work on your hiding skills."

He picks at the tool shelf.

"Listen, about Michelle . . . she dumped me, but I don't blame you—" I clear my throat. I take a step toward him. "We've been friends too long," I say.

He turns and growls at me like a wild animal, baring his teeth, shaking the tool shelf. As he steps into full view, I catch my breath. He's naked.

I back away and laugh uncomfortably. "Have you gone totally crazy?"

Joey staggers forward and shoves me against the door frame.

I smell alcohol on his breath. He plunges past me, babbling nonsense.

He's drunk. During the ten years I've known him, I've never seen him drunk. His dad is going to kill both of us if he finds out. Whenever Joey does something wrong Mr. Chancey assumes I'm in on it. Okay, so I usually am, but not this time.

I straighten up. "Hey, Joey. Let me help you. You need to sober up before your parents come home." I remember they were going to visit Joey's aunt in Atlanta. Sometimes they spend the night. Sometimes they don't.

I'm freaked out. Joey is acting seriously messed up, and it's weird seeing him walk around naked, like he doesn't even know I'm here. He turns, and his glance sweeps past me. He walks over to a corner, presses one hand against the wall, and leans forward. He pisses onto the floor.

I laugh nervously. "C'mon, Joey, that's disgusting. Get dressed and then we'll go into the house and get some coffee." He just keeps pissing. "Your parents can't see you this way. You're so drunk you don't know what you're doing," I continue helplessly.

Joey stares over his shoulder for what feels like forever. His eyes have the look of a maniac, and I feel like he hears me, sees me, but doesn't know who I am. I swallow hard. Sweat runs into my eyes. I don't move to wipe it away.

He mumbles something under his breath and shakes his head.

I squeeze the cell phone. I think about calling 911. I can make sure his parents don't find out he got drunk. Joey's eighteen. He'll probably just get his stomach pumped. He's probably binged enough to have alcohol poisoning. I saw someone die from that once in the emergency room.

He says something about aliens, but the words don't fit together.

"It's me. Clay," I say, louder now. "If this is a joke, you're dead."

The wind moves the curtains again. Joey walks toward the window. Struts, actually. Like he's imagining that he's a hero or a god or something. He swings the hoe at the window, and glass shatters.

I feel sick all over. That's it. He's gone too far. I punch in 911 on the cell phone. After two rings the operator picks up. "My friend is drunk and out of control," I say quickly. I give the address, keeping an eye on Joey, who is staring down at the shards of glass on the floor.

Then he turns and fixes his eyes on my face. He swings the hoe back and forth, trying to hit me. I run for the door. Joey screams, "Weeds, weeds, weeds," but I don't think he has gardening in mind.

I hear the 911 operator tell me not to panic.

Joey staggers to the door and faces me, swinging the hoe.

I freeze.

"Let me have the hoe, Joey," I say with a calmness in my voice that I don't feel.

He comes at me and hits my shoulder with the back of the hoe. I yell out as pain radiates down my arm. The phone and hoe go *whack-clang*, hitting the floor.

He mumbles something. He's so close I can see his bloodshot eyes, wild and dark. He grabs me around the neck. I'm gasping for air and trying to say, *"Please don't, please don't."* The words are a whistle as his fingers press my windpipe. I knee his groin, he doubles over, and I push him. He staggers. I hear a thud as his head and body hit the concrete floor. He doesn't move.

"Joey?" I call, my voice raspy as I swallow air. "Shit! Joey?" I crawl over to him, put my ear close to his nose and mouth. I feel his warm breath against my ear.

I roll onto my back and stare at the ceiling. What the hell just happened?

Joey makes a noise. I turn my head. Vomit runs out of his mouth. I jump up and turn him onto his side so he doesn't choke. After a moment he's all right. I'm pretty sure he's only passed out and vomiting from all the drinking he did today.

In the distance sirens wail. "Help's here, Joey. Don't worry." I feel relieved, but also more scared that Joey is really in trouble now.

Two EMTs enter, carrying a gurney and toolboxes. "My friend has been drinking," I say. "He went crazy. I pushed him and he passed out. His head hit the floor. He vomited."

"Move away, please," one of them says firmly.

I release Joey's hand, stand, and back out of the way. They kneel at Joey's side.

"Good carotid pulse," one says.

"Airway is clear. Respiration's good."

They connect him to a portable heart monitor and place a clip on his finger.

"BP one forty-six over eighty-eight. Oxygen saturation ninety-seven percent."

His numbers are good. I'm thankful for that.

I hear footsteps, and I turn my head. "Up against the wall," a police officer says. "I need to search you." Another officer walks around the room, peering into the corners, crunching over the broken glass in his heavy shoes.

"I haven't done anything wrong."

The first officer's hand grips my arm, his nails biting into my skin. He leads me over to the wall and pats me down. He takes my wallet and looks inside. I have a driver's license, a meal ticket from the hospital, and three dollars. "What's your name?" he asks.

"Clay Gardener," I say. I glance over my shoulder. Joey's still not moving. The EMT is placing a cervical collar around Joey's neck. I know that's just a precautionary measure they take with anyone who might have a neck injury.

"What happened?"

"I don't really know," I say, and tell him what I do know.

"Were you two drinking together?" he asks roughly.

"I just got off from work. You can check with the hospital that I was there."

"Right," he says skeptically. "Okay, breathe into this." The officer sticks a Breathalyzer in front of my face. I blow. I pass.

"Let's get an IV in and transport," one EMT says.

"Did he take any drugs?" the other EMT asks me.

"He doesn't use drugs," I say. "But this is really weird. He never drinks alcohol."

"Is he allergic to anything?" the guy asks.

"Not that I know about."

He opens a package, swabs Joey's skin at the elbow, and starts inserting a needle. The other EMT has a bag of IV fluid ready with tubing. He connects the end of the tubing to the IV catheter.

Joey starts moving his arms and kicking his legs, slowly at first, but then more vigorously.

The policemen help hold him down. "What the fuck?" Joey screams. "Help! Help!"

"Relax, Joey. Relax. They're helping you," I say, trying to look between the men surrounding him to find his eyes.

Joey turns his head toward me and quits fighting. Tears are running down his face.

"Let's move him while he's calm," the EMT says. "On three." He counts. They lift Joey onto a gurney and tie down his wrists. The EMT puts a plastic airway into his mouth and then an oxygen mask over his face. I know Joey's still naked under the sheet.

They carry him out, leaving wrappers and plastic needle caps behind.

The officers are nosing around the shed. One of them picks up Joey's pants and checks the pockets. I've got to find out what's going on with Joey. I want to go with him to the hospital. When the officers aren't looking my way, I tiptoe outside.

Saturday, 8:33 PM

The sun's gone down. The Chanceys' house is dark. My bike's lying knocked over on the ground. It's like my whole world got sick when I wasn't watching.

In the driveway the EMTs slide the gurney into the ambulance. I start to climb inside.

"You can follow in your car," one says.

"I don't have a car." I rode my bike here straight from work.

Sweat's running down the side of my face. "Couldn't you let me ride with Joey?"

He shakes his head.

"I've seen you around," I say. "I work at the hospital."

"Sorry. You should check with the officers to see if they need any more info."

I try to protest but he turns away. He climbs into the back of the ambulance, and the other EMT gets into the driver's seat. I run to my bike. The ambulance pulls away, lights flashing.

I grab my bike, get on, and pedal hard and fast, chasing the ambulance. I must look like an idiot. The ambulance pulls farther ahead until its lights vanish on the other side of a hill. I hear the approach of a car. I move to the shoulder of the road and stare straight ahead, pedaling as hard as I can. The car comes up behind me, passes with lights flashing, and pulls to the side of the road. I slow as the chief of police climbs out.

I stop. I know Chief Baker. I met him after Joey and I almost burned down the woods next to Joey's house when we were twelve. He looks as mean as ever. "Where the hell are you going?"

"To the hospital."

"You're riding a bike all the way to the hospital?"

I do it all the time. "It's a long walk."

Chief Baker's staring at me. I guess if I were brave, I'd be looking him in the eye. But I'm afraid. The cops at the shed treated me like a criminal.

"Can—may—I go now?" I ask. "Or are you arresting me?"

"You shouldn't have left the property. I need more information. How do I get in touch with Joey's parents?"

Calm down. Breathe slowly. "Joey's eighteen, so I don't see

17

any need to call them. He wouldn't want you to. Don't you have to keep some kind of confidentiality?"

"No." Chief Baker looks up and down the road.

My head's swimming. Joey's getting farther and farther away. "One of the policemen already has the info. He got Joey's wallet out of the pants next to the bed in the shed. Joey has three hundred dollars inside, a driver's license, and a card with emergency contact numbers that his mother made for him. I think the EMTs—"

"All right," Chief Baker says abruptly. He sits in the cruiser, makes a call, and gives the information.

"Where did he get all that money?" Chief Baker asks.

"Joey got paid yesterday. He works downtown at Ridge Pharmacy. He was going to buy some stuff for his dorm room. He's going to Duke next month. Premed." I rub my right shoulder where the hoe made contact.

"Was anybody else with Joey today?"

"I don't know. I've been at work at the hospital."

"Does he use drugs?"

"No. Never. He doesn't even drink." As far as I know, and I should know better than anyone. I touch my shoulder. It's hot where I got hit.

"Uh-huh. What's wrong with your shoulder?"

"I got hit with a hoe."

"Do you need to go the hospital and get an X-ray?"

"No. I need to go to the hospital to see about Joey."

"Get in. I'll give you a ride."

"You're not going to arrest me?"

"Not if you're telling the truth."

Holy shit. Somebody actually believes me.

CHAPTER 3

Saturday, 9 PM

We pass the ONE WAY sign for the road that winds around the hospital and see an ambulance backed up to the emergency entrance. Chief Baker pulls into the drive. My T-shirt clings to me. I unstick it from my chest, fan my armpits, and run my fingers through my tangled hair. "Let me out here," I say. I open the car door before he comes to a full stop and jump out. He pops the trunk so I can retrieve my bike and says he'll find me later to talk.

Twenty-seven minutes have passed since the EMTs slid Joey into the ambulance.

The waiting room is jammed full of patients with lacerations, headaches, stab wounds, ear infections, and bad coughs—a typical Saturday night. Things people think are emergencies. Some are. Some aren't. The admissions clerk is busy taking a payment from somebody. I want to run around searching for Joey, but I've got to take this slow. I have to calm down.

I stop at the water fountain and lap up the cold water. I'm so thirsty I could drink a toilet tank dry. I glance at the pay phone and think about calling Michelle, and then I suddenly remember. She's not my girlfriend anymore. I hate when stuff like that happens. Joey calls it mind zoning. He made up the term. You push something out of your mind temporarily to focus on bigger issues, but then when you remember, it feels like it just happened.

I drink more water. Out of the corner of my eye, I glimpse Mrs. Hunt sitting next to the clerk.

I go over to the desk and say hello. I know I look bad. "What are you doing back here?"

I lean over the desk. "I'm here to check on a friend, Joey Chancey. He was just brought in."

She flips through the papers and checks the patient census and shift reports. It must not be serious if she has to check. I wait for her to smile, to say he's in good condition. It's not like me to worry like this. Joey worries. He worries about school, grades, his father's corn that's dying from the drought. She doesn't even look me in the eye. "He's in stable condition."

Stable can mean anything. "Could I go back there and sit with him?"

"No."

I sigh. There's nothing I can do but wait. "What's wrong with him?"

"You should get any information from his parents."

Mrs. Hunt scares me almost as much as Joey's father. When she looks at me over the top of her bifocals, I feel like she's seeing a screw-up. Sometimes when I mess up, she fills out an incident report that I have to sign. And every time somebody makes a mistake or has an injury, they have to have a drug screen. I'm extra careful.

Once, Mrs. Hunt said I work like a hungry hound dog. I told her the only hound dogs I'd ever seen were always stretched out in the sun sleeping.

"Can you work tomorrow?"

"Sure. Seven AM to seven PM like today?"

"No. I just need you for eight hours. Seven to three."

I'll make forty-eight dollars before taxes. A lot of people would laugh at that. A lot of people wouldn't waste their time working for that. Joey wouldn't. He makes almost fifteen dollars an hour at the drugstore, but that's partly because his dad is old friends with the owner. My dad isn't old friends with anyone.

A little kid sitting next to the water fountain starts heaving. I run and grab an emesis basin from a shelf behind the check-in desk and put it in front of her face just in time. Mrs. Hunt brings a wet washcloth.

"It won't be much longer," Mrs. Hunt tells the mother. Her voice is kind.

The lady pulls the child to her chest. She runs her hand through the girl's hair. I see the kid wrap her arms around her mother's neck and close her eyes.

You're lucky, kid, to have a mom to hold you when you're sick.

The mom looks at me with gratitude in her eyes.

The intercom crackles. "Code blue, ICU. Code blue, ICU . . ." I feel a surge of adrenaline run through me. I almost forget I'm not working.

"Clay, could you . . . ," Mrs. Hunt says. She answers codes anywhere in the hospital. She heads toward the elevator and leaves me holding the basin of puke.

I love this place. Without looking at the basin, I take it to the dirty utility room. If Mrs. Hunt asked me to work all night I'd do it. Heck, I'd probably work for free if I could afford it. When I'm at work I feel like I can be anybody, do anything. Even if I'm just dealing with a puking kid, it makes a difference. I belong here.

It's the same good feeling I get whenever I walk into the shed. I bet I don't get many chances to do that anymore. I feel angry for a second that Joey has probably screwed up our situation with the shed. Most people our age don't have their own place to hang out. Now his parents won't trust us.

I go through the triage room to the patient care area. "Yo! Clay," Guthrie calls as I pass a room. "Bring me some suture, will ya?"

I empty the basin in the dirty utility room, wash my hands, grab the suture from the supply closet, and hand it to Guthrie.

"Thanks, Clay," she says. "I've been meaning to tell you that you did a good job earlier this evening."

I smile. "Do you know what room Joey Chancey's in?"

She shakes her head. "What's going on?" she mumbles so that the kid lying on the stretcher a few feet away doesn't hear. He's about eleven years old. He's holding gauze over one eye.

Guthrie loves to talk. Most of the time she's answering my questions. Like the other night she explained an EKG to me and how each blip should have PQRST waves and what each one means. She's pretty interesting.

"An ambulance brought him a while ago. We've been friends for years."

She shrugs and looks away. "Hang out a minute, will you, Clay? I'll check."

I nod. I'd stand here all night for information. I stuff my hands into my jeans pockets. The kid seems scared, and I'm wondering if I have the same scared look on my face. I smile at him.

"Are you an MD?" he asks. His voice squeaks like he's got a rock in his throat. With all the blood on the gauze, I figure he got hit in the head with a rock.

"Sure," I say. "If MD means that I'm momentarily detained, morally delayed, and mentally deranged."

The boy laughs like he's heard the funniest joke ever.

I glance at two pictures of a human heart on the wall. One shows how healthy it is on the outside. The other shows it cut open, with arrows pointing to diseased parts. It's interesting how you don't know what's inside a person until you look.

Guthrie returns. "Let's talk in a few minutes," she tells me. She covers a metal tray with a green sterile towel.

"What color stitches do you want?" Guthrie removes the gauze from the kid's forehead.

"How about yellow?" I say. "They'd look cool against the bruise."

"We don't have yellow," Guthrie says. She starts cleaning the cut across the top of the kid's eyebrow. He asks her why there are no yellow stitches.

"How about a yellow Popsicle instead?" I ask.

The boy gives me one of those kid smiles that make me feel

like I'm God. "Sure," he says. I swear, if I were him, I'd be screaming by now. He's a lot like Joey. Joey never complains. I don't either, unless it involves pain.

I get him a Popsicle from the fridge in the medication room. Inside there are tiny containers of juice that hold barely enough for one big gulp.

After I give him the Popsicle, I go over to the counter. Guthrie's stuffing prepackaged alcohol wipes into a drawer as she waits for a doctor to appear and sew up the kid. I ask her why his parents aren't with him. She says the father can't stand the sight of blood.

She faces me. "Do you know you have bruises on your neck?"

I touch my throat. I can't feel them. I shake my head.

"You need to stay away from your friend for a while."

Sometimes I forget how opinionated she is.

"Joey was hallucinating. He was calling for you. I like you, Clay, and I have no idea what's going on, but this makes you look bad. You know how everybody talks." She turns away. "Don't jeopardize your job. Get out of here. Go home. He's getting good care."

She thinks he'll make me look bad? Funny, after all these years of wanting to feel like I was good enough to hang out with Joey, somebody says he'll make me look bad.

"He was only drinking." I gulp. "He probably has alcohol poisoning."

"You don't see patients acting like that from alcohol. I'm sure he took a hallucinogen."

"You're wrong," I say flatly. I could list at least a dozen times I remember a misdiagnosis being made in the ER. "Thanks, though," I say as I leave the room.

I can't just walk away—not when Joey's calling for me. I stand outside the triage area and wait a few minutes until a nurse wheels a patient toward the treatment area. I step inside and take the white lab jacket I sometimes wear over my scrubs from a hook on the door. I calmly walk back out. A half dozen medical personnel stand around the nurses' station. No one looks my way. I keep walking like I'm working, and then stop and read the white board on the wall behind the desk. Joey's in the trauma room.

I walk into trauma like I'm supposed to be there and ease over into a corner. Joey's lying on the same gurney the girl died on a few hours ago. It's too weird watching somebody I care about get worked on by the doctors and nurses. He's not just some anonymous patient.

I never learned the dead girl's name. I wish I had asked.

I struggle to follow what's happening. A doctor inserts a central line into Joey's neck vein. Joey also has an IV in his arm. I can see his hairy legs sticking out from the sheet.

I screwed up, I suddenly realize. Anyone with half a brain would know something was wrong if they walked into a room and saw it torn apart. A normal person would leave and call for help, in case a burglar was hiding in the shed. How come I'm so stupid? Why did I wait to get help?

Joey's arms and legs start jerking. His head rolls back. "Seizure," the doctor says, then shouts an order for phenytoin and diazepam. I know phenytoin is used for seizures. Diazepam will relax him. My dad used to take it sometimes for anxiety.

I sag against the wall. My body gets cold. Why would Joey have a seizure? I've never seen a drunk in here having a seizure.

Green stuff runs out of Joey's mouth. The doctor suctions

him. "He's aspirating. Let's intubate." He stands at Joey's head and inserts a metal device into his throat. Somebody gives him an endotracheal tube. The doctor takes the plastic tube and slips it in.

"Throw me the ambu," the therapist says, and a nurse grabs the bag from the emergency cart and tosses it from the foot of the gurney. The therapist forces oxygen down the tube with the ambu. The respiratory therapist listens to Joey's chest. "Breath sounds good," she says as a nurse tapes the tube in place.

Joey's pale face grimaces and the tube sticking out of his mouth wags. I keep remembering the sad, desperate look I caught in his eyes as the EMTs tied him to the stretcher back at the shed.

Any minute now I could burst apart. But I force the feeling down into my gut and swallow hard. It can't be that bad, I tell myself. I'm remembering the girl from earlier and that's making things look worse than they are. Joey isn't like her. She was crushed in an accident. He just partied too hard. The medical personnel keep working on Joey. I would switch places with him if I could.

"We don't need any more help," a nurse says to me suddenly. She looks at me like she smells a fart. I glance at Joey and move around the outside of the group like I'm leaving. I can't go, though. I feel like if I stop watching, something bad will happen to Joey.

The doctor's inserting another tube into Joey's nose above the one already sticking out of his mouth. The respiratory therapist is attaching the bottom tube to a breathing machine. Now the doctor is using a giant syringe with the tube in Joey's nose to pump out green stomach contents. At the counter behind him a nurse is preparing the mixture of activated charcoal that will go in Joey's stomach.

I move to the head of the gurney and stand behind the doctor. "Don't forget to get a CT," I say. The doctor looks over his shoulder. "Who are you?" he barks, but I'm already backing toward the door.

The charcoal is supposed to bind to the remainder of the drug so it can pass through Joey without problems. They think he overdosed. Overdoses are treatable. We see at least a couple every week. This is no big deal.

I lean against the wall outside the trauma room. I don't know what to do when I've already done too much.

Saturday, 11:30 PM

Two hours have passed since I left the trauma room. I'm sitting in the waiting room with my head resting against a chair arm. My mouth tastes like stale coffee. The lab jacket is folded under my head and my eyes are focused on the emergency department entrance. The Chanceys haven't arrived yet. I rehearse what I'm going to say when they come in. I'll tell them everything I know, which is basically nothing. I'll stay calm. I'll keep my eyes focused on Mrs. Chancey because I don't think I can handle Mr. Chancey's glare right now.

In my lap I'm holding a medical textbook for EMTs. I looked up alcohol poisoning and seizures. I looked up hallucinogens. I looked up head injuries. Joey's symptoms match everything. They even matched some stuff in the "Complications of Pregnancy" chapter.

"You can see him for a few minutes," Mrs. Hunt says. I look

27

around. She's standing a few feet away. "He's somewhat awake and stabilized. We'll be taking him up to the ICU as soon as a bed is set up."

I nod. "Thanks." I try to smile. "I figured you'd be gone by now."

"Busy night." She touches my hand. "I can only imagine how worried you are about your friend. Look, why don't you take tomorrow off? Don't push yourself so hard."

"No. It's fine. I can do it." I want to be here.

"You should get some rest."

"I will."

Sleep is overrated anyway.

I take the medical textbook with me to read later.

I open the trauma room door and peek inside. The room is lit up like it's the middle of the day instead of late at night. Joey's eyes are closed. "Joey," I say softly. My heart's running faster than the heart monitor on the stand above his bed. A bag of D5NS hangs from a pole, and an IV machine pumps at 125 cc/hr. The tube in his mouth hitches up his lip on one side. At the side of the gurney a ventilator breathes for him.

I take a hard breath of hospital air. Maybe he isn't as bad off as he looks. I place my arms on the metal side rail. "Joey, wake up." I reach out and touch his arm. It's moist and warm and sticky. I hold his hand, and his fingers, speckled with dried-up blood. He squeezes back. His eyes open and reveal cloudy, dilated pupils. His lips move.

"You can't talk because of the tube," I say. "I can't stay long. They'll be transporting you to a real room in a few minutes." It's kind of crazy. If I were working tonight, I'd be the one getting the bed ready for him.

The machine whooshes like ocean waves. Joey digs a fingernail into my palm. "Paper," he mouths around the endotracheal tube. "Paper." His eyes water.

I unclench his hand from mine and pat his arm. "Be right back," I say, and wipe my eyes with my forearm.

At the nurses' station, I get a pen, clipboard, and paper. The nurse on the phone doesn't notice. She's giving a report to somebody on the other end of the line about Joey. She's saying, ". . . altered mental status, possible alcohol poisoning and/or drug overdose. He's oriented now but groggy. Alcohol and drug screen aren't back yet. He was intubated and placed on a ventilator after a seizure to protect his airway. His oh-two sats were in the eighties but are in the upper nineties now. Vital signs are stable. His CT was normal. . . ."

I breathe in relief. A CT is the same thing as a CAT scan. It's a special kind of X-ray. It would show a head injury if there were one.

I go back to Joey's room and untie his right hand. As he writes, his hand shakes, but he's sober now. He gives me the clipboard. The words are faint, scraggly lines on the yellow paper.

Don't tell anything. Tell doctor to only talk to me.
I know president.

"You mean you know who the president is?"

Joey nods.

I laugh a little. I bet somebody asked him ten times if he knew the date and who the president is to figure out if he was confused or not.

His parents will be upset if nobody will tell them anything. They'll expect me to give them every detail. "I'll tell the nurse," I say. "That's all I can do. I'm not sure it's right. Your parents will see you and know you're not here for a checkup." I hand the clipboard back to him. "What's the big secret? You aren't the first person in the world to have too much to drink."

Explain when I can. 2 hard 2 write. Head hurts.

"Just tell me one more thing. Did something else happen? I don't understand any of this. The shed was a wreck. Who else was there with you?"

The breathing machine blares. Joey struggles to breathe against the ventilator. He shakes his head fast. Water in the plastic tubing rattles. I hear the heart monitor beep faster and faster.

"Breathe with the machine, Joey." From instinct, I match my breathing to the respirator's. Joey lies still as the ventilator gives him a deep breath, then another. His heart rate drops and for a few seconds I'm afraid it's going to keep slowing until all that's left is a straight line. But his heart rate returns to normal.

Joey was class valedictorian. He was voted most likely to succeed. I was voted the most likely to pedal a bike the rest of my life. There's a picture in the yearbook of me on my bike next to the cafeteria Dumpster with the caption TWENTY YEARS FROM NOW.

Joey played football because he wanted to be well rounded for college. I got a job at the hospital because I've dreamed about being a doctor most of my life, and I'm usually desperate for money. My dad expects me to pay half the rent, half the utilities, and half the grocery bill. That takes almost my whole paycheck.

Joey shakes the side rail. I look over at him. A tear is running down his cheek. He writes:

Ck Champ.

"Sure." I bite my lip. I don't remember seeing Joey's dog anywhere around. I can't think about him right now. I squeeze Joey's hand. "I saw Champ when I was at your house," I lie. "He's fine. He'll be fine. I should tell you, I called the ambulance. The police came. I talked to Chief Baker. Everything's cool."

Joey's eyes get wide.

"I didn't feel like I had a choice. If you only knew—"

The respirator and heart monitor alarms. I show him how to breathe, and I rub his forehead.

"Sorry," he mouths. "Sorry."

"You don't need to be sorry. I'm sorry I was jealous before. I don't care about Michelle. You were right when you said I deserved the Golden Asshole award."

He holds on to my hand.

Mrs. Hunt hurries into the room with a syringe. A respiratory therapist, an orderly, and two nurses follow her.

"This will relax you," she tells Joey, and sticks the needle into the rubber port of the IV. She glances at me. "You should go. We're ready to take Joey upstairs."

Joey keeps shaking his head. "Wait, wait, wait," he's mouthing. Sweat gleams on his forehead.

"Joey doesn't want any medical information shared with

anybody," I tell Mrs. Hunt. I show her the clipboard and what he wrote.

"You have that right," she tells him. "But no promises. It depends." She gives him a smile and touches his forehead. "Your parents are here now." She eyes me like she's trying to warn me. "I'll let them see you as soon as you're settled into your room."

"Rest now, Joey," I say. "We'll talk tomorrow."

Joey lies limp, but he has tears in his droopy eyes. I lean down and whisper, "I'll find out what happened today."

He shakes his head. He mouths, "No."

"Okay. Whatever you say." I place the clipboard on the foot of the gurney and head toward the door. The side rail clanks, the respirator blares. I turn. Joey lifts his hand. He waves goodbye.

CHAPTER 4

Sunday, 12:10 AM

Mr. and Mrs. Chancey stand at the admissions desk in the ER waiting room. They haven't noticed me standing in front of the triage room, building up my nerve. Mrs. Hunt touches my shoulder.

"They'll be asking you questions," she says. "You're not the person to give them answers. I want to remind you about patient confidentiality."

I nod. Charlie, another orderly, got into trouble once in the cafeteria when a doctor overheard us talking about a patient. We weren't gossiping or anything. Charlie was telling me how to change the bandage on the patient's ass, but he accidentally said the patient's name.

I tuck my T-shirt into my jeans. I take a step toward them.

I force calmness into my voice. "Hello, Mr. Chancey, Mrs. Chancey."

"Can you tell us anything?" Mrs. Chancey almost shouts when she sees me. She's wearing a coffee-stained white shirt and black pants. The night I first met her, I was seven years old and my head barely came up to her waist. I used to pretend she was my mother.

"Did you talk to the doctor?" I say, looking around for a doctor to speak to them. "I'm not allowed to discuss patients, even though it's Joey."

"No, nobody has told us anything except there was an emergency, he was brought here, and now he's being moved somewhere," Mr. Chancey says, hunched over the counter like a broken old man. His necktie hangs like a noose around his neck. "Thank you for getting help for Joey in time. We didn't know he was sick when we left the house this morning."

He doesn't know a lot of things. I nod. I can't look him in the eye. I take a deep breath. He smells like Old Spice. Sometimes I feel lucky that my dad barely knows I'm alive. I can do whatever I want, whenever I want. Other times, I feel like I've missed out on something important.

Like the night Joey received the Student of the Year award, I noticed the look on Mrs. Chancey's face. She cried giant tears of happiness. I couldn't stop staring at her then. Nobody's ever going to cry or shout with joy for me.

Mrs. Hunt appears and tells the Chanceys that the doctor will speak to them now. They forget about me and follow her.

At the elevator I stare at the closed doors. I bang on the Up button.

• • •

I ride to the second floor. It's weird how much you can learn just by riding an elevator a dozen times a day. Reading the signs helps distract me from my thoughts. A "Patient's Bill of Rights" hangs next to the panel. I've memorized the key words— dignity, respect, privacy, confidentiality. A doctor doesn't have to tell family members anything unless he deems it is in the best interest of the patient.

I get off the elevator and take a right down the deserted hall. In the daytime it's filled with administrators and coordinators and committee people. I ignore a CLOSED sign and enter the cafeteria.

I dig in my pocket and find eighty-two cents, enough for a Coke from the machine. I go to the table at the back next to the window, behind a large pillar.

I sip the Coke. The cafeteria is like a giant empty refrigerator, gleaming silver and silent except for a distant hum. I read through the symptoms of alcohol poisoning again: mental confusion, stupor, coma, vomiting, and seizures. It says a person can pass out, choke on their vomit because the gag reflex is impaired, suffer permanent brain damage. It's important to get help right away. Letting someone sleep it off can be a death sentence.

I rest my head on the table. My eyes start getting heavy, and my stomach's growling. I eye the vending machine full of chips and candy, but I don't have any more change.

The hospital intercom crackles to life. "Clay Gardener, dial the operator. Clay Gardener, dial the operator." Surprised, I sit up. The switchboard operator wouldn't know if I was working or not. Only two people have ever called me at work and one of them is upstairs on a breathing machine. It has to be Michelle.

She dumped me to go after Joey. I don't know how much encouragement she got from him. That was something I wanted to talk to him about.

I can't deal with her now.

I open the book again. My twelfth-grade language arts teacher—any of my former teachers—would pass out if they saw me now. Who'd ever believe that Clay Gardener was in a hospital cafeteria after midnight reading a book without pictures?

Sunday morning

I can't sleep. All night I wait for the sun to rise. I'm glad my shift's only eight hours today.

The cafeteria finally opens at six and I use my meal debit card to get a giant cup of coffee with cream and sugar. I sit at my table and drink it slow. When I'm finished, I force myself to get up. My head's swimming, but I'll be fine in a couple of minutes, after all that sugar gets into my bloodstream.

I shower and change into scrubs in the doctors' lounge, where I keep deodorant and toothpaste in my locker. That's all I need, but some clean underwear would be nice. I have to remember to do laundry. I take out the stethoscope Joey gave me for Christmas and hang it around my neck.

After I clock in, I head to the ICU to check on Joey, but I get paged to the intermediate care unit on the fourth floor. The nurse tells me to check vital signs. Thirteen patients later I'm almost finished when I hear "Dr. Strong, CCU" over the intercom, which means they need people who are strong to respond. I don't feel very strong today, but I have to answer.

A naked man's standing in a puddle of urine and blood. He's

ripped off the monitor wires and pulled apart his IV connection. Blood drips from the IV catheter still stuck in his arm. He's screaming and swinging his pillow over his head like a lasso.

"Delirium tremens," a nurse says. "Can you believe he told us he didn't drink?"

I put on gloves, grab a sterile 4x4 bandage and tape from the dressing cart, and rush into the room to the man's side. I grab one arm. "Take it easy, man," I say. I can't do much about the bleeding from the IV catheter except hold the bandage over it until I have help to get him under control. Charlie arrives and takes his other arm. The man's still shouting.

We ease him back toward the bed. He sits. Charlie lifts his legs while I hold on to his shoulders. We whip him around flat onto the bed. A nurse appears and pulls the IV catheter the rest of the way out, slaps gauze onto the man's arm, and tapes it down. He's cold and clammy.

He calls us names and screams about snakes crawling up the wall. We apply leather restraints. The nurse reconnects him to the heart monitor and gives him an injection.

Snakes are popular hallucinations. I don't know what I'd see if I hallucinated, but I know it wouldn't be snakes. I like snakes. The first time I witnessed delirium tremens, the patient believed she was in a bar. She thought her IV was a martini. She drank the whole thing, never mind that she had to squeeze the bag to squirt the stuff into her mouth.

Until then, I thought I'd seen everything that could happen in a hospital. But I still get surprised by stuff here.

I wonder what Joey was imagining yesterday when he attacked me. It must have been terrifying.

I look over and spot this boy—he's maybe fourteen years

old—peering at us through the window of the room. I bet I had the same look on my face yesterday as I watched the doctors intubate Joey. I take off my gloves, pull the curtain around the bed, and step out of the room.

"Hey," I say.

"Is my dad going to die?"

"I think he's going to be okay. You should wait in the waiting room," I say. "Somebody will come out and give you an update. It looks a lot worse than it really is. Your dad just needs some medicine to help him get through this."

I spend the rest of the morning delivering supplies, taking specimens to the lab, passing out lunch trays, and then, an hour later, picking them up. I don't take time to eat, and I've forgotten to be hungry, I'm so busy. I wash my hands a couple of dozen times. Sometimes they get so dried out and red that they sting.

It's almost time for me to get off when I head to the ICU to see Joey.

Joey's eyes are half open, and his long lashes are matted with sleep. Mucus rattles inside his breathing tube. I automatically turn my head toward the TV. A woman on some talk show says, "These people here today have cheated death."

Cheating has nothing to do with dying. Cheating's easy. Staying alive is hard. If death could be cheated, everybody would be doing it. I cheated a few times in the third grade. I'd write notes on the bottom of my shoes, and I wasn't caught until the day Joey saw a picture of the southern United States on my right sole. He told me I had Mississippi and Louisiana backwards. That was sure something. Knowing where Mississippi and Louisiana were when the ink had already smeared.

I change the channel to cartoons. Bugs Bunny wallops Daffy with a hammer.

I turn and face Joey. He lies there, the machine controlling his breathing. He smells like sour towels. "Hey, Joey," I say. "I can only stay a few minutes. I have to go home." I'm hoping he'll be able to talk to me today, or at least write something again. I walk over to him and pinch his arm. Fear creeps over me. I can hear his heartbeat on the monitor, but he looks dead.

Why is Joey unconscious? I go into the hall and see Jan, the charge nurse, inside a room, working with another patient. I wave to her. She nods. She'll come as soon as possible.

I go back into the room and take Joey's hand. I watch him and wonder why he's not responding at all. This can't be from alcohol poisoning. He was writing notes to me last night.

The blood pressure cuff inflates and deflates. It reads 152/96. That's a little high. His oxygen level reads 89 percent, which is way too low. My oxygen level was 98 percent last time I checked when I was playing around with the pulse oximeter in the ER.

His heart rate speeds to 175. Spit bubbles from his mouth. Alarms on the ventilator and heart monitor sound. I grab the suction tubing and start cleaning Joey's mouth. That's why his oxygen level is so low—he's not getting much air through the tube. "Hang on," I tell him. "Hang on." I don't suction inside the tube. I haven't been trained to do that.

Jan runs into the room. "He needs oxygen!" she says sharply.

I drop the suction tube and throw her the ambu bag. She connects it to his breathing tube, and I turn the oxygen on the wall up all the way. She nods and begins squeezing the bag to push air into Joey's lungs.

After a few breaths he's improved and the alarms stop.

She reconnects Joey to the ventilator. "His tube was clogged," she says.

She writes down his blood pressure and his heart rate and checks his pupils. I'm picturing me suctioning Joey's mouth when he already wasn't getting enough oxygen.

I swallow hard. "Did I do the wrong thing?"

Her lips tighten. "You did fine. You did all you could do."

"Has he had something to knock him out?"

She keeps writing. "He's been medicated," she says vaguely.

My hands shaking, I wipe Joey's mouth with a tissue. A patient's condition can change in an instant. I remember a guy who was brought into the emergency room in full cardiac arrest. He'd participated in a triathlon, crossed the finish line, and passed out. The doctors thought it was heatstroke or a heart attack, even though the guy was in his twenties. Later I learned that he had a head injury. That's what the autopsy showed, anyway, but nobody ever knew for sure how he received the head injury.

Jan leaves the room.

I hear the clock on the wall ticking. I pull one of Joey's eyelids up and peer at his pupil. Then I check the other. They're unequal. Pupils are supposed to be the same size. I decide to hang out awhile to make sure his breathing tube doesn't get clogged again.

I sit in the chair at his bedside and I'm not sure why, but I start thinking about his pet fish.

When Joey and I were kids, he had this betta fish that lived in a small bowl in his den. One morning we went in to play video games and found the fish floating. The water was green and slimy and smelled like a toilet. Joey filled a glass with distilled water and put the betta in. "You're wasting your time," I told him. "Trust me," Joey replied. The betta floated lifelessly for hours. Then that afternoon I happened to glance at the fish. I saw its gills moving, and I stared at it for a long time, whispering to myself, "I can't believe this." A moment later the fish started swimming around the glass. I swear it had been dead. The fish went on to live a very long time. Joey said the fish was special because it beat the odds. I kept shaking my head in amazement. I believed that Joey had brought the fish back to life.

I take a deep breath. I can see why Michelle wanted him and not me. It makes sense. I grip the chair arms and watch my knuckles turn white.

Jan comes into the room with a couple of other nurses, a respiratory therapist, and Charlie. "We're taking him to CT," Jan says.

"What?" I say. "Another one? The one he had last night was normal."

"This one is just a recheck," Jan says. "Nothing to worry about."

I stand and grab the head of the bed. I want to help.

Jan touches my arm. "We have enough help, Clay. Isn't it time for you to go home?" She lays Joey's chart on his bed with him.

I let go. I wish I could do something. I wish I could read his chart. I think she's avoiding telling me something.

They pull the bed out of the room. Jan's winding the monitor cord around her hand, but it feels like she's winding it around my chest. I can't open my lungs. I can't get a deep breath.

"Clay," she says. "You're too involved with this case. I don't want you in here unless you've been assigned to do something. Go home. Joey's in good hands."

I nod. I'm relieved. I thought she was hiding something bad from me, but she's just concerned that telling me anything is wrong because I'm Joey's friend. Jan's one of the best nurses in the hospital, and she rarely loses a patient. She's employee of the month at least a few times a year. Her patients are always sending her chocolate.

Sunday, 3:15 PM

It probably doesn't matter, but I do it anyway. First I go to the nurses' station and stand at the counter pretending to look at my assignment sheet. I've got to hurry. One nurse is on the phone. Another is at the door of a room talking to Dr. Finemann. I slip into the conference room next to the nurses' station. My heart's beating hard and fast. I take a few breaths. Please don't let me get caught. I ease the door shut and pick up the phone to call the lab.

"This is Dr. Finemann," I say, trying to sound professional. "What was the alcohol level on Joey Chancey from last night? It isn't on his chart, and I can't get to the damn computer. I need the drug screen results, too."

"Point twelve," she says, after a few seconds. "I don't see the drug screen."

"Thanks."

Confused, I hang up the phone. Joey never had alcohol poisoning. He was drunk, but .12 isn't that high.

Okay, Gardener, I'm telling myself. You don't know what's going on. You feel guilty, but Joey was already hallucinating when you arrived yesterday. You didn't set him off. He was already in trouble, seriously messed up. You just have to figure out why.

There are about twenty kids from the high school standing around outside the waiting room, whispering amongst themselves or hugging each other like they're in shock. Alicia and Wade are in front of the bathrooms. It hits me that the therapists and nurses went past here as they took Joey to CT. I wish they hadn't seen Joey the way he is now. Not Joey, the invincible. Not the class valedictorian who won the Outstanding Student of the Year award.

I head in the other direction to clock out.

The kids from high school have never had much in common with me, even less so now that they're all just weeks away from college. They wear hundred-dollar jeans and drive new cars. They throw parties and invite Joey, and I sometimes tag along with him, when I don't have to work. But even when I'm there, I'm not there. I'm always on the outside looking in, wishing I had a car, wishing I had money, wishing I had a life.

CHAPTER 5

Long Ago

I never knew my mother, but I remember her from the stories my sister, Darcy, told me. Darcy's stories made her real to me. On the day I was born, Darcy and Dad were in the waiting room when they heard the emergency called in labor and delivery. Darcy got cold all over, and she heard a voice telling her to take care of Miriam. "Who was Miriam?" I asked Darcy.

Darcy smiled, and her eyes lit up. "You were supposed to be a girl."

Something happened after Mom received an epidural, something that almost never happens. She quit breathing. Then her heart stopped. The doctor did a cesarean section right there in the bed while everybody else was doing CPR on her. I was born a few minutes after her heart quit.

I was in the hospital for almost three months. Just about

everybody knew me, Darcy said. The day I went home, Darcy carried me down the hall, and over the intercom a voice said, "Clay Gardener is leaving the hospital today."

Darcy took me outside where a limousine waited, provided by the hospital. She was proud that day, and she said she loved me as much as a mother could love a child. I wish stuff like that were imprinted on my brain. I'd like to be able to remember riding in a limousine and all those people who saved my life saying goodbye.

For years Darcy read to me every night. She thought I might have brain damage because I didn't talk until I was three and nobody ever understood what I was saying until I had speech therapy. Darcy said she believed reading to me all the time would make me smarter.

My dad, Darcy, and I lived in Endurance, Texas, until I turned seven. Darcy was a senior in high school planning to go to college when the warehouse where my dad worked burned to the ground. I was sitting in his lap in the La-Z-Boy and Dad was tracing letters on my back. Through the living room window I could see darkness coming, but we were inside, safe and warm. Then a special report on television showed a fire at a warehouse. I felt my dad stiffen. I turned and looked at him. His face grew pale, and I felt scared. But I didn't realize until a few days later that our life in Endurance had been destroyed along with the building. The owner decided not to rebuild and declared bankruptcy. My dad didn't even get his final paycheck.

But it was a good thing it was a Sunday. The building was empty. How lucky was that?

Dad sold our furniture. The owner of our house came by and said if we were moving we needed to pay him the back rent we owed. Dad said we weren't moving, just cleaning out some old things. Then he took us out for ice cream. When Darcy and I were settled in the backseat with our ice cream cones, Dad announced we were going on a road trip. He drove back to our house and loaded a few things in the trunk. Next thing I knew it was morning and we were in a roadside park next to the interstate. He told us about his friend Clarence Chancey. They'd been in Vietnam together, and Dad owed him a visit after all these years.

While my dad talked Darcy and I ate powdered-sugar doughnuts, one of my favorite foods in the world.

We drove for three days. The heater in the car didn't work, and it was winter. Winter in the South is relatively mild, but it can still get really cold at night. Some nights were so long I thought they'd never end. I worried about frostbite. Darcy told me you could only get frostbite in the snow, and she held me when we slept.

Our van finally rolled to a stop in Georgia, in front of a house with reindeer on the roof. "You wait here." Dad looked at the reindeer and smiled for the first time in a while.

"Oh, great," Darcy mumbled. "They're going to love us for showing up on Christmas Eve." Her cheeks were as red as Christmas lights.

I slid into the driver's seat, stuck my head out the window, and gazed at the reindeer on the roof. They looked alive. Against the starry background, they were magic.

Dad came back to the car grinning. "Come on. We can get warm inside." At the front door a scary man dressed as Santa went, "Ho ho ho."

I started to run the other way. Dad grabbed my arm. "This is Clay and Darcy."

"I am so happy to finally meet you after all these years." The man gave me a big smile. "You aren't scared of Santa, are you?"

I was scared of men who dressed up in red suits.

Inside I saw a giant Christmas tree with a million presents stuffed underneath. "How come you aren't wearing a jacket?" a kid said. He peered out the door at us from behind his dad.

I looked down at my dirty T-shirt, at the hole in my jeans, at my tight-fitting sneakers without the shoestrings. "I never get cold."

"So how come you're shaking?"

I shrugged. I didn't know what to say.

"My name is Joey. My dad says you can be my new brother, if you want."

My dad laughed uncomfortably. I wondered if he was giving me away.

We ate leftover Christmas Eve dinner while the kid and his mom and dad watched us like we were exhibits in a zoo. When I took my plate into the kitchen, I heard Mr. and Mrs. Chancey talking in another room. "They're pitiful and dirty," she said.

"I wish they'd come sooner," he said.

I went back into the dining room. Joey was showing Darcy card tricks.

"Washing off at the gas station didn't do any good," I told Dad. "They said we were dirty."

Dad smiled sadly. "They're right, kiddo. You need a bath."

Mr. and Mrs. Chancey came into the room. "We have a place out back fixed up for you," Mr. Chancey said. "We'd like you to stay, and in a couple of days you can see about that job."

"It's the shed," Joey said. "My dog, Goldie, sleeps there."

"It's not a shed," Mr. Chancey said.

The shed, or whatever it was, was awesome. One side of the room had a sink, a counter, and cabinets. There were bunk beds and a couch along the wall across from the sink. In the center of the room a frilly cloth and a vase of flowers decorated a wood table. A small heater warmed the place. A giant toy crate sat in the corner.

"Oh my God," Darcy said. "They have a big house, and we have to sleep out here."

"You're crazy, Darcy," I said, pulling GI Joe from the crate. "This place is great."

I got to sleep warm and safe on the sofa with Goldie snuggling and scratching against my back, kind of like she was holding me. I felt good, the way I used to feel when I'd sit in my dad's lap and he'd scratch letters on my back for me to guess.

The next morning, Christmas, Joey gave me a blue jacket and a red toy bus he'd gotten from London. "I hope you don't mind wearing my old jacket," he said.

I held the jacket in my hands. It was the best I'd ever owned. "It isn't old. It's a collector's item."

"What do you mean?"

"Worn by somebody famous."

"I'm not famous."

I shrugged. "You probably will be someday."

• • •

48

We spent the next week playing pool in his basement and building the Empire State Building with dominoes in the shed. Mrs. Chancey was trying to take Darcy under her wing, so they spent hours in the kitchen. Darcy looked annoyed the whole time. "Why do you get to putz around the basement while I have to slave away as Betty Crocker's assistant?" she asked me one night as we brushed our teeth. I just shrugged. I liked the brownies and pot roasts and other stuff Mrs. Chancey made for us.

Early one morning, Dad shook me awake. "It's time to go. I found an apartment, and I have a good job."

"Doing what?" Darcy said in a sleepy voice from the top bunk.

"Driving a garbage truck."

Darcy groaned. I thought it was a cool job, but I shook my head. "I don't want to go."

"We have to go, Clay. We don't want to depend on anybody."

"I want to tell Joey goodbye."

"No. They're all asleep. I thanked them last night. Besides, we'll be seeing them again soon."

We moved into the apartment, which was bigger than the shed but not as fun. A couple of days later I rode the four miles to Joey's house on my bike. I had planned the route with a map I'd found in the phone book. I slowed before I got to the corner of the yard, and I watched. I hoped Joey would see me. I hoped he wouldn't. He didn't come outside and I didn't know if it would be okay to knock on his door, so I didn't. I rode out there every day for the next week. Sometimes I'd park my bike in the cornfield across from his house and watch. Some people might say I was stalking him, but I didn't know what stalking was.

One day Joey was finally in the front yard. He saw me and waved. I went over and asked what he was doing. "I'm digging to the center of the earth." His eyes lit up as he smiled. "Where you been?"

"Around," I replied.

"Your dad lets you ride your bike all the way over here?"

"I always went everywhere on my bike when we lived in Endurance."

"Where's that?"

"West Texas. It's thirteen hundred miles from here. It took us three days to drive, but we stopped a lot." I got on my bike. He asked where I was going. "Just down the road," I said, because I didn't want him to think the only reason I'd come over was him.

"Why? There's nothing that way but a dead end."

"I'm in training. One of these days I'm going to bike cross-country to the Pacific Ocean." I said it like it would be easy. "I'm going to stop off at my old house in Endurance and see who's living there."

"Cool," he said. "Can I train with you?"

I said yes. His mom said no. "I want to do what Clay does," he said.

"I'll watch him," I said seriously.

She smiled and looked at us for a few seconds. Finally she nodded. "Okay, you watch him."

We rode our bikes down a gravel path next to the two-lane highway. Mrs. Chancey stood on the edge of their front yard. I wasn't used to having an adult keep an eye on me, and there wasn't any traffic—just fields and trees along the road. Joey and I pretended we were riding to the other side of the world. We rode right over any valleys, mountains, and rivers that blocked the way.

The next day we added another domino to the Empire State building that we had started before I'd left. It collapsed in less than ten seconds. Then Joey told me about a movie he had watched with his dad. Two cowboys who had saved each other's lives decided to become brothers. They cut their palms and held them together, mixing their blood.

"Should we do it?" I asked excitedly, looking around for something sharp to cut ourselves with.

Joey looked squeamish for a second. "Naw," he said, "it doesn't have to be actual blood."

He found an empty Dr Pepper bottle, and we spit into it. He explained that spit has a lot of the same stuff in it that blood does.

"Now we're blood brothers," he said as we stared at the bottle. Then he told me he wanted to go with me on my cross-country bike trip.

We spent the next ten years planning.

CHAPTER 6

Sunday, 3:30 PM

It's four miles to my apartment from the hospital. Usually I'm grateful to leave work, but I'm not looking forward to the ride home in this heat. Plus I wanted to stay, to keep an eye on Joey, but there are things I need to do in the morning.

At the QUIET HOSPITAL ZONE sign nailed to a metal post at the corner, I stretch while I wait for the red light to change. I glance toward the emergency room to see if there are any ambulances outside. There aren't. Then I look up at the roof to see who has snuck up there to smoke. I see a couple of employees by the railing. The roof is supposed to be off-limits. A nurse jumped once. I heard she'd left a note saying she'd made a terrible mistake. Her ghost haunts the roof now, searching for redemption. I remember the nurse, actually. She could calculate milligrams per kilogram of body weight in a flash in her head during a code. She was smart, like Joey.

The light changes. I pedal hard and fast. At least the feeling of the wind against my face wakes me up a little.

I pass a car lot with a homemade sign that reads, USED CARS. BUY NOW—PAY LATER.

I wish I had a car. Nothing fancy, just something to keep the bugs out of my mouth and the rain off my head. I already have a driver's license with the required stupid picture. I stare straight ahead. A car's not that important. I'd rather have a touring bike. The lightweight one I want costs two thousand dollars.

I rotate my right shoulder. It doesn't actually hurt so bad.

I ride on the edge of the road. I'm always careful on my bike, just in case a drunk driver or someone using a cell phone comes along. A delivery truck roars by and shakes the ground. As I pass the Biggs County Animal Shelter, dogs howl. I imagine I've just escaped from a prison and the dogs are after me.

The thermometer on the Biggs National Bank reads ninety-nine degrees. It's hot even for a late afternoon in August. Most of Georgia hasn't had rain for a month, and Dr. Dobie, the disc jockey on the country music station Joey and I like, predicted the worst drought in fifty years. Not many guys our age listen to country music.

Hot and sweaty, I open my front door and push my bike into the apartment. The phone's ringing like crazy. My dad's at his usual post, asleep on the sofa. I drop my bike and grab the phone.

"Finally," Darcy whines. "I've been trying to call you since last night. Where were you?"

"Work." I flop in the La-Z-Boy and stretch out my tired legs. "I'm planning a nap. Can I call you back tomorrow?"

"No," she says. "I was worried about you, and I'm auditioning tomorrow."

I figure she's just feeling lonely again. Darcy moved to Nashville a few years ago to become a country music star. She's twenty-seven now. She's not a star yet, but she is a bartender at a country music bar. She can make any kind of drink imaginable, and she's fast.

I haven't seen her in forever, and I miss her. She couldn't even make it to my graduation. The biggest night of my life and her fan belt broke before she got out of Nashville. Dad came. After it was over, he shook my hand and told me he was "real proud." But he hadn't planned anything special for me, so I went to a restaurant with Joey and his parents.

"You're supposed to wish me good luck," she says.

"Good luck," I say.

"It doesn't count when I have to tell you."

The one and only time I saw Darcy audition she wore a long black skirt. She looked like a fat black olive and when she stepped off the stage she tripped on her hem.

"I'm too tired to think," I say. "I've seen the sun rise every day for two weeks now. It gets old."

"What's going on? You do sound awful."

"Joey's in the hospital."

I hear silence. "Why?" she asks finally.

"I went over to his house, and he was acting crazy and drunk." My mouth is dry. I get out of the chair and head for the kitchen, holding the phone against my ear.

"God, it's just like the Chanceys to take Joey to the hospital for getting drunk. Their precious Joey."

"I was the one who called the ambulance. People die from alcohol poisoning." I open the refrigerator and pull out a Coke. I guess I should prepare her. "But he doesn't have alcohol poisoning, and I might be in trouble," I say. "The police came."

"Were you drinking with him?"

"No," I say. "When I found Joey, he was already drunk, and he was acting crazy. I had to push him to get him off me and I might have hurt him. Mr. and Mrs. Chancey don't know I pushed him."

I hear her suck in air and let it out slow like she's blowing out cigarette smoke. "It's a good thing you called the police. That's proof you weren't the one who caused the trouble."

"I don't think anybody filed a report."

"Even better," she says. "If it were serious, they'd file a report."

"And I passed the Breathalyzer test," I say.

"Okay. Good."

"But Joey had a seizure at the hospital. He was all right afterward."

"Jesus Christ."

"It's not that bad," I say. "He'll probably be taken off the breathing machine tomorrow."

"He can't even breathe? Clay, how serious is this?"

"Everything is under control."

"Shit, Clay," she says. "Don't you know you could get charged with assault and battery?"

This from someone who's learned criminal law from watching

Court TV. "All I can do is tell the Chanceys what I know. I'm going to figure out the rest."

"What are you going to figure out? There's nothing to figure out. Just don't get involved any more than you already are. You need to stop hanging on to Joey all the time," Darcy says. "You need other friends."

"I have other friends." I hope she doesn't ask me to name them.

"You have Joey's friends," Darcy says flatly. "Has anybody but him ever invited you anywhere? Has anybody but him ever come over to play with you?"

I laugh. "Sure. Everybody's beating down my door to play with my toys. Hold on. I'll wake Dad."

I go over to him and start shaking his shoulder. "Darcy's on the phone," I say. "Wake up." He moans and says, "Okay, okay," before turning the other way. He starts snoring.

I sigh hard. He's always been this way. When he's not working, he's sleeping. Somehow he still finds the time to get fat, though. Once in elementary school I called him to pick me up after a school play. For the next hour I plucked dandelions from the yard in front of the school. He finally arrived. He said he'd been putting his shoes on to come get me and fell asleep in the chair.

"Stop snoring," I yell at Dad.

"Don't do that," Darcy says. "He works hard."

"Not that hard."

"He could have put you up for adoption."

I almost hang up on her. She's always throwing that in my face. Like everyone was doing me a big favor by not abandoning me after I was born. It's not like my dad even took care of me, anyway. It was Darcy who did everything for me until I was eight years old. Then after she ditched me for her illustrious career I had to take care of myself.

"I want to move," I tell Darcy. "I can't stand it here. I'll never be able to save enough money for college or my bike trip. Dad charges me for food and rent. I think he charges me for the air."

"That's life. People pay rent." She snorts. I feel like I'm talking to a farm animal. What does she know? She hasn't lived here in nine years. I take a slug of Coke. My lips tremble. She's right about Joey being my only friend.

"How's—uh—what's her name?" Darcy asks.

"We broke up."

"Why?"

"Because I don't understand girls. One day she likes me and the next—well—she doesn't." I shake the Coke hard enough that it foams over the edge.

"I told you she was using you," Darcy says.

"Listen, remind me to never tell you anything again." I lick the foam off the can.

"You know you love my advice."

"Sure, why don't I just put my whole future in your hands, Darce?"

"I could help you go to a trade school. You're good at dealing with people. Dad says you're the best orderly at the hospital."

How would he know? The time Darcy auditioned wearing that black skirt, Dad said she was beautiful, but I was embarrassed to be seen with her. "I don't want to go to a trade school. I want to be a doctor, not an orderly forever."

"Clay, people like us don't go to medical school."

That kind of hurts.

When Joey was accepted to Duke, I was jealous. He was—he is—going to be living my dream.

"You could've been a great violinist," I say. "Or a singer."

"Yeah, me and a thousand others." Her breathing's ragged, like she's about to cry. "Sometimes what you want isn't what you get," she says.

"I bet you won't even go to that audition tomorrow."

She lets out a sob, and I'm thinking, Don't do this to me. Don't make me feel bad because things haven't happened for you.

"I didn't mean to hurt your feelings," I say when I hear the phone click. I listen to the buzz coming across the telephone line, and a hollow feeling swells up in my chest. I ease the receiver into the cradle.

"Hey!" I yell to Dad. "Hey!"

Dad rolls onto his side. Yawning, he sits up.

"What's wrong? How come you're so tired?" I snap.

"I was up early this morning. Then I helped some neighbors move." He rubs his shoulder.

"Oh." Now I feel bad for yelling at him.

"I got you a book." He nods toward the coffee table.

I pick it up. The title is Camping Across the United States. The price sticker on the front says $29.95.

"Thanks." I run my finger across the price. "You shouldn't have paid this much."

"The people moving were giving away some of their things," he says. "I also got some clothes that'll fit you."

I sigh and lay the book on the coffee table. "I need your help."

"Okay. Okay." His eyes are almost closed.

"Joey and I had an argument yesterday. I pushed him, and he hit his head."

"That's too bad," he says. "But I'm sure Joey won't stay mad at you." He stands and turns on the TV. He picks up the remote. "What do you want to watch?"

Jesus Christ. He doesn't even give me a chance to finish. "It wasn't just a little fight," I say sharply. "Joey's in the ICU."

His eyes widen and I'm kind of glad that I shocked him.

Dad reaches for the phone on the end table. The light on the answering machine's blinking.

"What are you doing?" I ask.

"Calling Clarence Chancey to find out what's going on."

"He won't be home. I'm sure of it. I'm trying to tell you what's going on. He doesn't know—"

Dad covers the receiver with his hand. "Be quiet, Clay. He's home."

So Joey's doing better. He has to be if his dad left the hospital.

I listen while Dad talks. All he says is "Uh-huh" three or four times. He hangs up the phone.

"Well? What did he say?"

"He wants you to get your stuff out of their shed," he says, sounding defeated.

I chew my thumbnail. "What else did he say?"

"He said he won't have you bringing beer to his house anymore."

"I didn't!" I stand up. "You know I'd never do that. Why didn't you stick up for me?"

"He's upset about Joey right now. He isn't thinking straight."

So I get to be the scapegoat.

Dad rubs his eyes. "He's always been very proud of Joey. He has a problem believing that Joey would do anything wrong. He'll calm down once Joey is back home." He manages an expression of vague sympathy and reassurance, but mostly his eyes just look tired. "Want something to drink?"

I show him the drink in my hand and he trudges to the kitchen to get himself one. Times like these I feel like screaming. He's an okay dad, but he's simple in a way. He never gets that some situations require solutions more complex than sitting back and letting things settle down. He's never understood that I like to have—that I need—a couple of dollars in my wallet. He's never understood why going to college is important to me. Once he made me calculate how much I could make in eight years by working instead of going to college and medical school. He thought that was a fortune. I told him ignorance costs more than learning. He got mad. He said I was putting him down.

I open the camping book and thumb through it. My dad returns to the couch and turns the volume up on the TV. He's got some good points. I've always done whatever I want to do—as long as money wasn't needed—and he's never asked me, "Do you have any homework?" When I was younger he never made me take a bath or brush my teeth or get my hair cut. He didn't even get upset with me for almost burning down the woods behind Joey's house when I was twelve.

Joey decided we needed to learn to camp so we wouldn't have to stay in hotels when we biked cross-country. We'd sleep under the stars. "We're looking for an extreme survival challenge," he said.

"We are?" I answered.

We used a tarp we found in the shed for the tent. We made a campfire and squirted lighter fluid on it. The tarp caught fire. So did a tree and a bush. We ran back into the house and Joey called 911. Chief Baker arrived about the same time as the fire department. We got a lecture. At first I was scared he'd take us to jail, but he smiled and said he used to love camping.

As punishment Mr. Chancey put us to work digging a garden and planting tomatoes, cucumbers, and corn. The ground was hard and rocky and the hoe blistered my hands. I turned brown and got strong. By late summer we had a lot of vegetables. Joey and I set up a roadside stand. Chief Baker would stop, buy something, and leave us a tip. The profit made us feel rich. Joey came up with the idea of giving fifty percent of our earnings to a firefighters' charity and saving the other half for our bike trip. I could have used the money myself, but I didn't want Joey to think I wasn't a good person.

After Dad goes to bed, I check the messages on the answering machine. Most of the calls are from Darcy, telling me to call her. My heart stops when I hear Joey's voice. It's scratchy sounding, like he's a million miles away. The answering machine's old—my dad found it in somebody's garbage a long time ago. I replay the message and lean down to listen.

"Hey, Clay. How come you aren't at the party? Pick up the phone. You still mad at me?"

There's a lot of noise I can't figure out in the background before the tape goes silent. I don't move. I didn't know anything about a party.

CHAPTER 7

Monday, 6:45 AM

I'm feeling all right when I wake up. I got some good sleep. I know my dad's already gone to work, but I didn't hear him leave. Right away I start thinking about Joey and the message he left. I listened to it a few more times last night as I tried to piece together what must have happened. Joey got wasted at some party and everyone ditched him when he started acting weird. There's nothing wrong with partying, but there's something wrong when people abandon someone who's really messed up. Especially when those people are supposed to be friends.

I'll get my things from the Chanceys' today. I was planning to go the shed anyway, to look for some clue about what happened to Joey and to feed Champ. I lie in bed, and for a minute

I try to pretend that this will be any other day. I'll go to the shed and Joey will already be there, looking over some new piece of equipment or a map we'll need for our next bike trip.

Two and a Half Months Ago

Joey and I biked across the state during our April spring break. Before our trip he ordered maps from the Department of Transportation and spread them out on the floor of the shed. He planned every turn and every stop along the isolated county roads.

To get ready physically, Joey and I took turns lifting his bike, bags, and equipment over his fence and carrying it a hundred yards. We camped in the woods behind his house a few nights. Every two hours his mom or dad would call him on his cell phone, I guess to make sure we hadn't been attacked by a bear or killed by a psycho murderer.

The night before we left I had a dream that I was on the highway and a girl in a red car came along and offered me a ride. She drove into the woods and took off her clothes. Then I woke up yelling, "No!" I don't know why I always wake up when I get to the good part of a dream.

I remember how we stood in Joey's front yard next to our bikes. The panniers and racks held our stuff. The sun was rising, and my lids were drooping big-time. It was really early, but Joey didn't want to waste any daylight.

"I don't like this idea," Mrs. Chancey said, as if we hadn't gone over our plans with her a dozen times.

"It's dangerous," Mr. Chancey agreed.

Joey turned to me. "Tell them we know what we're doing. They'll listen to you."

"My dad isn't worried," I said. "And he taught me how to use pepper spray."

Mrs. Chancey moaned and put her hand to her chest.

"Clay was joking," Joey said, eyeing me.

Mr. Chancey wanted to follow us in his car. You'd have thought we were seven years old and going around the world. Joey promised he'd call every few hours.

We zigzagged northwest to follow the hilly county roads, rough with potholes that could swallow a possum. In fact, we saw a lot of possums, and I learned firsthand what their insides look like.

"We need a cause when we bike cross-country," Joey said when we stopped at a gas station to get boiled peanuts and use the bathroom.

"How about roadkill prevention?" I said.

But Joey came up with cancer research, the homeless shelter, the humane society, and about a hundred others. There were too many to choose from.

Two hours into the trip, a scary-looking black dog chased us. I was thinking about using the pepper spray when the dog ran directly in front of my bike. I swerved and landed in the drainage ditch at the side of the road. It contained a lot of interesting stuff, including a twin mattress and a toilet seat.

I picked myself off the ground and sat in the tall grass. I shuddered. "You okay, Clay?" Joey called.

"I'm peachy," I said. "Where's the dog?"

"You only stunned him for a few seconds. He ran home," Joey said. "You scared him."

The road got hilly after a while, and I started getting tired. Joey told me to ride behind him. It would be easier without the wind hitting me directly.

At lunchtime we stopped at a country café, and a guy sitting at the counter with another man looked us over. "Where y'all headed, dressed like a couple of circus clowns?"

We got our barbecue sandwiches to go. Back on the road I told Joey he shouldn't have worn his yellow and blue spandex biking shorts. Mine were at least a solid black.

After a couple of miles we pulled into the woods and sat under an oak tree to eat. I told him about the dream I'd had about the girl in the red car, and he told me he was still thinking of a cause to support. I was getting tired, and Joey's butt was hurting him, but we ate, rested, and got back on our bikes. We rode down dirt roads breathing dust, we rode through a thunderstorm, and we got chased by more dogs and then a rooster. I never knew a rooster could run so fast. We kept going.

After about eighty miles I thought I was going to die. I ate some chocolate, and the sugar high got me up the two-mile climb to the log cabin Joey had reserved for us. When I saw the place, I whooped, jumped off my bike, and lay down right in the middle of the road. Joey and I had biked eighty-four miles that day—the most we'd ever done at one time. When we opened the door of the cabin I'd never felt so relieved in my whole life. Whoever said riding a bike is easy never rode eighty-four miles carrying forty pounds of supplies.

I gave Joey some baby ointment for his burning ass, laughing because he didn't know that wearing underwear under your bike shorts causes major chafing. We both stank so it was lucky the place had a shower. For dinner we fixed hot dogs—the best I'd ever tasted. Then we tossed our sleeping bags onto the beds, and even though I was dead tired, we talked for a while about the other trips we'd take before the big one across the country. During the night I woke once to the sound of rain hitting the roof. It was a nice sound, almost musical. Kind of like the opening theme for bigger and better things to come.

In the morning we rode into a small town for breakfast. A restaurant, a gas station, and a school were arranged around the one intersection with a traffic light. I didn't see any other businesses. Joey and I devoured big plates of eggs, country ham with red-eye gravy, and grits. The grits were free, and I figure we got our money's worth. After eating, we went outside and asked a farmer to take our picture in front of the restaurant, only he couldn't figure out how to use the camera.

"This is heaven," Joey said. "I can't wait for the cross-country trip."

So we set a date. There in the parking lot of Mom's Diner and Antique Shop we decided we'd leave in six weeks, on June 1, right after graduation.

Monday, 9:30 AM

In the bathroom I wash my face and wish I had some of Darcy's makeup to cover the circles under my eyes. I dry my face, practice smiling in the mirror, and look at my teeth. Back in eighth grade, the dentist recommended braces, but I didn't get them. I open my mouth wider. My teeth look straight enough to me.

I'm calculating how much money I can save working forty hours a week at a little more than minimum wage. I'll have the money for the bike trip, college applications, *and* braces if I can work a few extra hours each week for the next few months.

Michelle, Joey, and I have only one thing in common. We all wanted to have fun this summer. Both of them got new cars for graduation, they both have living parents still married to each other, and they both spend money like the supply's endless. One time we talked about allowances, and the two of them agreed that five hundred dollars a month would be enough pocket money for college. I was speechless. But I'm not sorry I work at the hospital. Even if I didn't need the money I'd do it.

I grab the phone in the living room and dial hospital information. The lady tells me Joey's condition is listed as guarded. To me, "guarded" conjures an image of policemen standing outside the room. I expected her to say his condition was fair or even satisfactory. You don't get tubes taken out and go home when you're in guarded condition.

But "guarded" is all right. "Critical" is when you start worrying and call family members and the preacher and close friends. You could also call that "grave."

Somebody knocks. I look through the peephole and see the apartment manager. Vic's a tall, skinny guy around the same age as Darcy. He always wears tucked-in golf shirts and khakis. When Darcy visits, she goes out to dinner with him.

Okay, Gardener, I'm thinking. You don't know why he's here, but you're almost sure it's because the rent hasn't been paid. Turn on that smile and pretend it was an oversight. This is not the first time your dad has forgotten.

"Hey, Clay," Vic says.

I get weak in the knees when I see Chief Baker leaning against the stairwell a few feet away.

Vic lowers his voice. "I'm just showing Chief Baker which apartment is yours. I thought I'd pick up the rent while I'm here. Are you in some trouble?"

I shake my head.

I go to the kitchen counter, take my checkbook out of the drawer, and write. I know my dad will pay me back when I tell him. I think about all the questions Chief Baker could be waiting to ask me.

"Thanks," Vic says when I give him the check. He talks louder. "You and your dad have been good tenants for ten years."

"Vic," I say, hoping Baker doesn't hear. "He knows you did that on purpose."

"It's all right," Chief Baker says with a half nod. "I was going to ask anyway."

"You want me to stay?" Vic asks, because he likes Darcy. Maybe he thinks that makes him my big brother or something.

I shake my head and look over at Chief Baker.

He's dressed in jeans, a T-shirt, and a cowboy hat. I guess he's off today. Looks like he hasn't shaved. He rubs his chest and then his left arm. Beads of sweat line his lumpy forehead.

"Want to come inside?" I ask, and open the door all the way.

As he passes me, he takes Rolaids from his shirt pocket and swallows a couple.

"Is Joey all right?" I ask as he sits on the couch with a heavy sigh.

He wipes his forehead and takes a few breaths before answering. "I'm going over there as soon as I'm done talking with you."

He starts asking the same questions I answered before. I know it's part of his job. He wants to know why I was at the shed yesterday. I talk about working my twelve-hour shift at the hospital and then coming over to see Joey.

"Who else would be likely to visit Joey?"

I shrug and rub my shoulder. The bruise is black today. "Just about anybody. All I know is that there was a party during the day. Joey left a message for me telling me to come. I just heard it last night."

"Does he normally have parties when his parents are out of town?"

"Never. And it wasn't necessarily his party. He just went to one."

"Uh-huh. Who have you seen hanging out with Joey?"

"I don't really know. The usual, I guess." I mention Wade and Alicia.

He asks me about a couple of people I've never heard of. I only know most people from our senior class by sight. I shake my head. "Maybe they were at a party, but I don't know. No one has talked to me about it."

He nods. "Did you feel threatened yesterday?"

"I got hit with a hoe," I say. "And I value all my body parts." I meet Chief Baker's eyes. "I don't care about that. Joey didn't know what he was doing. He's a straight-A student. He's going to Duke, and he could've gone to Harvard. He's going to be ashamed this happened. I wish his parents didn't need to know." I start to get choked up.

Chief Baker looks away like he's embarrassed, or maybe he remembers seeing Joey and me cry that day we almost burned down the woods.

"Let me ask you something just between us," he says. "Wouldn't you want whoever gave Joey alcohol to be prosecuted?"

I look down at the carpet and see a bug turned upside down wiggling its legs like it's trying to run. "No," I finally say, clearing my throat. "See, I know Joey better than most people. He wouldn't want somebody getting in trouble for something that everybody does. He'd feel guilty."

Chief Baker nods. "Which is better than dying. Are you sure he never used drugs?"

"He never did. He wouldn't. Why? Did something show up on a drug test? It's wrong if it did. I've seen lab reports get mixed up. I even know of a person who got the wrong blood transfusion." I pause and look around our shabby apartment anxiously. "I think you need to be looking for real criminals."

"This is in relation to another investigation. Do you know where to buy marijuana?"

"I have no idea," I say. "I don't know anything, and Joey doesn't either."

"Nobody's going to be charged with anything in Joey's case. I'm just trying to find out who's been selling alcohol and drugs to kids."

"I swear I don't know anything."

"Do you like Joey?"

I nod. "Of course. But I don't know if we'll be friends anymore after this." My voice breaks when I say it and I look down at my feet in case my eyes tear up.

"Why?"

My stomach twists. "I don't know."

I watch Chief Baker rubbing his chest and then his left arm.

He's sweating, and he looks like he could fall over and die right here.

I take a deep breath. "You having chest pain? You should get checked," I say, trying to sound professional. "Overweight men your age are high-risk for heart attacks." He stares at me. "Not that you're overweight."

"It's heartburn," he says. "I had burritos for breakfast."

"You could get checked in the ER since you're going there anyway."

"You seem eager to get me away from here," he says with a look like he's just swallowed antacids flavored with bull.

I glance at my watch. "Most people die within the first thirty minutes of a heart attack. You probably have plenty of time. You've only been here five minutes." I look him in the eye. "Your face is red. I bet you have high blood pressure."

"I'm fine." He pushes himself up from the couch. "If you have any way of getting me a list of the people at that party, I'd appreciate it," he says as he heads for the door. I watch him walk down the hallway holding his wrist with his other hand, checking his pulse.

CHAPTER 8

Monday, 11 AM

I'm getting out of the shower as the phone rings. I grab a towel and drip all the way to the living room. Mrs. Hunt asks me to work from 7 PM to 7 AM. I have to do it. I can't say no. It still gives me time to get stuff done this afternoon. I've got to go to Joey's house to get my things and feed Champ. I also have to talk to Michelle and find out what she knows. She would never miss a party. Maybe I can still make things work out for us. Maybe all this stuff with Joey will throw everything into perspective. She'll realize she needs me more than she needs parties and fun. And I sure could use her right now. Without Joey around, I feel like a lone traveler in a country where I don't speak the language.

Monday, 11:30 AM

I'm excited and anxious as I pull my bike into the half-full parking lot of the funeral home. Michelle lives with her parents on the second floor. There's a separate entrance around back with stairs leading to a porch. I've never been invited upstairs. I've never met her family. Not too long ago, I knocked on their door without calling first. Michelle answered and told me her parents didn't like anybody just stopping in. They like to keep the place really quiet for their clients.

I met Michelle in eighth grade. We had language arts together. I used to watch her prop her hand under her chin and stare out the window. Sometimes she'd suck on her pencil and then drop it. I'd pick it up. She'd do it again and again and again. I was like a dog waiting for a treat. She never talked to me. I loved her anyway.

After winter break she didn't come back to school. I heard a lot of rumors: She had been kidnapped. She'd run away with an older guy. Her parents had sent her to boarding school. I never forgot her.

Two months ago I walked into the service entrance at Hamm's funeral home to drop off a deceased patient's dentures. As I was headed in, she was coming out with a Fredericks of Hollywood catalog. "Michelle? Is that you?" She looked me up and down. I was wearing scrubs and a stethoscope around my neck. "I'm—I'm Clay Gardener. We took some classes together in eighth grade."

Her face changed from scorn to a slight smile, and then I thought I saw excitement. "Oh my God! I can't believe it's you! I didn't recognize you because of the scrubs. You look great."

One point for me. I looked good.

I gave her the denture cup and said I'd brought the teeth so that nobody would have to return to the hospital to pick them up. She took them, asked me to wait, and came back a minute later.

We sat on a stone bench in a wooded area across the parking lot. It's a place for mourners to meditate or smoke. She told me she'd been sent to a private school in the Northeast because the schools in Georgia were shit. She had graduated and was home for the summer break before starting college. She lit a joint and offered it to me. I told her we have random drug tests at the hospital and I could get fired.

"Too bad. This is good stuff. From New York." She took a long drag and winked at me.

After that, I'd stop after work to meet her almost every night. I'd listen and watch her twirl her hair around her finger as she smiled at me and looked me directly in the eyes like I was the most important person in the world. She told me about her parents and their strict rules and the weird kids at boarding school. She talked a lot. I think she was lonely, now that she didn't know any of us from school.

Today I stop at the side of the building, get off my bike, and head to the wooded area. There are several people smoking cigarettes, but Michelle's not among them. I guess I have to go inside the funeral home. My heart gets a burning feeling like somebody cut a hole in it and poured in peroxide.

Michelle once told me about the night a side door was left propped open with a rock and a bird got inside. You wouldn't believe how much trouble a bird can cause in a funeral home. I think she was joking around, but she looked serious.

I open the wooden door, walk into the funeral home, and

stand inside the lobby feeling weird because I'm dressed in biking shorts. There's a chapel directly ahead of me. On the left is a hallway. An office and conference room are on my right. In the corner three people sit in chairs. A smiling man—too young to be Michelle's father—in a black suit asks if he can help me. I tell him I'm looking for Michelle. He says I can wait in the office where I'll be more comfortable. I doubt that.

I sit on a fat sofa beside a desk that faces a window, hoping she shows up right away. The sunlight's streaming through the window. On the opposite side of the room is a door. I'm betting it leads to the embalming area of the funeral home. I thumb through a casket catalog on the desk while I wait. I think the shiny steel ones are the creepiest.

After about fifteen minutes, Michelle comes into the room carrying a box. I stand and put the catalog on the desk. She looks good and that makes me more willing to grovel. She's dressed in a snug silvery shirt, a black jacket, and a black skirt. She gives me the smile that takes my breath away, the smile that makes me sweat and stutter, the smile that makes me crazy and makes me forget how heartless she can be.

"What are you doing here?" she says.

"You called me a couple of nights ago, at the hospital, after Joey was admitted. Why?"

She shrugs. "You should have come to the phone if you wanted to know." She shifts the box around in her arms and asks me to open the door. It leads to a corridor. "Listen," she says. "I'm really busy. I'm sorry you got the wrong idea about us, but when I go to Vassar, I'm walking out of everybody's lives."

"No problem." I force a grin. "Want me to carry that for you? It looks heavy."

75

She glances toward the corridor and grins at me in a way that makes me sorry I asked. "Sure," she says. "I don't think we have any remains at the moment."

"Remains?"

"Bodies," she says.

I gulp. I've been to the hospital morgue once, but the still-ness here makes everything feel scarier. I go into the corridor. She shuts the door. I follow her down the hall. I can hear my heart beating in the silence.

"I called Mrs. Chancey today. On her cell phone. She hasn't left the hospital at all."

"What did she say?"

"Hardly anything. I told her not to worry about Joey, that my dad was on a breathing machine after his heart bypass. There's nothing to it. She didn't seem to appreciate my opinion very much. I was only trying to make her feel better."

"Yeah, that's like you," I say. "Reassuring."

"I am. You can ask anybody here."

"Like who?" I ask. "The people in the caskets?"

She hits my shoulder in a playful way.

"So any idea what happened to Joey?" I ask.

"He got drunk. Some dumb-ass doctor needs a new car and put a couple of tubes into him."

I hope she never needs heart surgery, because the doctor wouldn't be able to find it.

We stop in front of a plain-looking door, and Michelle takes a key from the pocket of her skirt. She unlocks the door and we step inside.

I stop breathing. The space looks like an operating room. There's no cadaver in here, thank God. Though Michelle is pretty cold-blooded. I smell formaldehyde and see two metal tables with porcelain surfaces. A mechanical lift perches on the ceiling. Hoses line the wall and above them a black and yellow sign warns, CAUTION. I turn my head and take in a sink, cabinets, anatomical charts, and a door plastered with DANGER signs.

Michelle takes the box from me and sets it on a counter.

"Where does that door go?" I ask.

"It's a receiving room. There's a garage next to it."

"Why all the signs?" I ask.

"It's required by law." She reaches in her skirt pocket, takes out a joint, and sticks it into her mouth. "For any area of potential contamination from germs."

By this time I'm more interested in the joint in her mouth.

"What?" she says.

I don't know if she's kidding around with me or not. "Are you trying to kill us both?" I say with a nervous grin. "The chemicals down here are flammable."

She takes the joint and holds it in her hand. "I've done it before in the corridor. Nothing ever happened."

"What about the signs?" I ask.

She pulls a lighter out of her pocket and lights up. "Those danger signs are on everything, even the washing machine. I don't pay attention. Everybody else smokes cigarettes down here."

I'm betting everybody doesn't. "Were you at that party on Saturday?" I ask.

She leans against the counter, takes a drag, and exhales smoke. "You mean Alicia's?" she asks, and I nod. "Nope. I was working, and I can't stand her anyway. You can ask my dad if you don't believe me."

I believe her. "I remember your dad," I say. "Didn't he come to the school for career day once?"

"In eighth grade. Everybody acted scared to talk to him."

"I wasn't. Neither was Joey."

She laughs. "People kept kidding around that he was the Grim Reaper."

I'm beginning to understand why she's so cold sometimes. She's around death all the time. The one thing that scares most people is part of her daily routine.

"Want to come to my room after I'm done smoking?"

I glance toward the way out. "What about your parents?"

"Busy."

I look into her eyes and remember how she kissed the back of my neck the night after Wade's party. I kissed her neck in return, then her shoulders, and almost every inch of her until I didn't know anything else. But Michelle looks older today, tired. I think she's stoned by now.

"You're staring at me weird," she says. "You don't like how I look?"

Yeah, I still like how she looks. I don't like this place. "You look all right," I say.

She touches my chest with her hand. I wish I could forget I'm with a girl who's offering herself because she's stoned.

"Want a hit?"

"I'm working later," I say in a shaky voice.

"It wears off fast."

I can see it now—riding my bike down the highway stoned, weaving into traffic. "So did you hear anything about the party?"

"You're obsessed," she says, waving the smoke away from her face. "Forget that you weren't invited. It was just an oversight."

How does she know I wasn't invited?

She takes another toke. "I don't think you should be asking questions about that party. Alicia called me. Both Wade and she think you could have done something to Joey for revenge."

I lean against the counter. "Why would I do that?"

"Because you're jealous of Joey and me, that we had this connection. They said you can get drugs from the hospital easy and could have drugged Joey."

You'd think if Joey and she really had such a great connection, she'd act like she cared.

"I can't get drugs. The hospital keeps records and counts on all the dope."

But there's always a way. A nurse I knew fainted one evening at work. Later I heard she'd been giving one of her patients half of the morphine ordered for pain and then shooting up the other half. I'm not supposed to, but I've counted narcotics with another nurse before. I've discarded syringes of drugs left at the bedside when all the medicine wasn't needed.

"You smoke a lot, don't you?" I ask Michelle.

She giggles. "No more than anybody else."

She puts her arms around my waist.

I start thinking about how she dumped me to go after Joey. "I thought you said it was over with us," I say finally. "You're only doing this because you're stoned." I'm talking and she's sucking on my neck. I put my hands on her shoulders and push her away.

She shrugs. "Your problem is you're fixated on Joey. You

always have been. He's got more money, more friends, more everything, and he wanted to be with me. You got left out. It wasn't a big deal for Joey or me, we were just having fun. You're the one who freaked out."

"Joey said nothing was going on between you and him—"

"Whatev. If that's what you want to believe." She blows smoke into the air.

My legs are shaking. "And I've never freaked out," I say. "Not until I saw you in the parking lot with that guy."

Michelle shrugs. "So what if I was talking to a guy? I have other friends. You came over, and I talked to you. I'd do that with anybody."

"You'd do a lot with anybody," I say.

She turns away from me, walks over to the sink, and tosses the joint.

I cross the room and exit into the corridor. I don't stop until I'm outside. A funeral procession is pulling onto the street. There must be a hundred cars. Some dead guy had a lot of friends.

CHAPTER 9

Monday, 1:15 PM

I'm riding my bike back to my apartment to get a couple of aspirin for my headache. This day is starting to suck big-time, and it's still early. I tell myself that Michelle's just running her mouth. Joey told me on Friday that Michelle had been coming on to him. I had a hard time believing him, and now it sounds like he lied to me, like maybe it was more mutual than he let on. I tell myself it doesn't matter anymore.

I pedal faster. My breathing is rapid, and I'm building up a sweat. She makes me want to keep pedaling down the road forever. The more burn I feel, the better. I hear a car behind me blowing its horn for me to get out of the way. I move to the shoulder. The car passes too close to my bike and a girl yells out the window, "Hey, idiot. Stay out of the way!"

I raise my hand to give her the finger but my bike wobbles and I almost fall over. My face is on fire.

At home I open the medicine cabinet and take three aspirin. I turn on the cold water and splash some on my face.

I check the answering machine.

"Clay, I'm waiting to talk to you," Mr. Chancey says.

And I'm waiting as long as possible to talk to him. I bite my lip and dial hospital information. Joey is still guarded.

I should try to make a list of people at that party for Chief Baker. Alicia and Wade are probably Joey's best friends after me. They were Mr. and Ms. Congeniality of our senior class. Alicia was ranked tenth in our class. Wade and I didn't have a rank. When you're that far down on the list, the school officials don't like to say anything about how stupid you are.

Wade played football with Joey. Everybody was sure Wade would get a football scholarship. Then he injured his knee. He's working with his photographer father now and brags about the wedding receptions and all the free booze he gets to drink. He's sort of going out with Alicia, but he doesn't actually admit to that.

"Hey, Clay-Dough," Wade says when I call him, and I get this image of him pounding a hunk of clay. "Alicia said you'd been arrested."

"Are you kidding me?" I sputter. "I didn't do anything to be arrested for, and I don't like anybody talking a lot of shit. How would she know anyway?"

"She lives close by. She saw you with Chief Baker Saturday night."

"He gave me a ride."

"I heard you were at Joey's and you had a fight with him."

"Yeah," I say. "I missed the party beforehand. Did you have fun?"

"Damn. I missed a party," he says, laughing. "I had knee surgery the other day. I'm in a lot of pain. I can't even limp to a keg of beer."

But he would crawl for free beer. Suddenly I'm not in the mood to waste time calling Alicia. I've figured out nobody's going to tell me anything, and I've got more important things to do.

Monday, 1:35 PM

I call Joey's house. Nobody answers. Good. I've got to get my things and look around before his parents come home. I've got to feed and water Champ. He's probably starved to death by now.

Champ's a healthy golden retriever, nothing like the runt Joey and I delivered five years ago. I had come over to help Joey build a robot for a science project. Joey's parents were gone. Champ's mother, Goldie, decided it was time to birth her puppies in the shed.

After she'd had two puppies, she kept pacing in a circle. When I looked close and saw what was wrong, my curiosity turned to horror. One unborn puppy was still halfway inside her and wasn't budging. I looked at Joey, and he took off running. In a few seconds he was back with some rubber gloves he'd greased up with corn oil. He gave them to me.

"No . . . no way, Joey," I stammered. "I don't know how."

"Sure you can." His voice was shaking and tears lined his eyes. "You have to try. She likes you better than me." Joey called

83

the vet on the cordless phone we kept in the shed and relayed the instructions to me.

I inserted two fingers on each side of the puppy and gently rotated. Nothing happened. "Come on, Goldie, you got to do some work," I said. The whole world became quiet as I focused on the puppy.

When Goldie looked around at me again, her eyes were big and black and sad. I kept talking as I worked until the puppy was free. Goldie started licking the puppy, which we later named Champ.

"You did it. I knew you could," Joey said.

Like it was the most normal thing in the world to do, Goldie gobbled up the afterbirth and finished licking the puppies clean.

Joey and I watched them for a long time. "I'm not going to want to give them away," Joey said as the puppies went searching for their mama's tits. "Do you think something like a smell or a feeling could be imprinted in your brain forever and you'd never know where it was from?" He looked at the puppies. "Like them. After I give them away would they recognize their mom if they ever saw her again? Or me? Wouldn't it be great if we could remember everything that ever happened to us?"

I said yes. I had a hard time remembering to do my homework. That was the day I started thinking about becoming a doctor.

I hurry out the front door pushing my bike. The sun beats down on the apartment building's parking lot, and the sky is clear. Mr. Chancey's been praying for rain. He planted his corn a few months ago, but it's dying from the drought. Gardening is just his hobby, but he takes the corn seriously. Usually by this time it's almost ready for harvest. Joey and I have helped him every fall. It's part of getting in shape for our bike trips.

The dirty little kid sitting on the curb could've been me a few years ago. He's throwing a tennis ball into the air and catching it. I wave to him. Like always, he jumps up and runs over to me. "Can you play?"

I smile. "Not today, Andy," I say. I've played basketball and catch with him a few times. When Joey's over, we play dodgeball or football. It's like he thinks Joey and I are kids. I'm on the edge of promising him I'll play tomorrow when I stop myself. Sitting around waiting for somebody to come over or call is the worst thing in the world for a kid. I always used to sit and wait for Dad to get home from work. Sometimes I'd count the cars as they passed on the highway. I'd guess that when I counted twenty cars, he'd pull into the drive. I got good at math. I'd subtract the number of trucks or multiply the number of green cars and divide by the number of white cars.

"Are those your underpants?" Andy says, looking at my shorts.

"Cycling shorts," I say. "I wear them when I have to ride my bike a long way. Sometimes I wear regular shorts over them."

"Without underwear?"

I nod. Smirking, he says, "Then those are your underpants."

I guess he's right.

CHAPTER 10

Monday, 1:45 PM

I pedal fast toward Joey's house, my backpack straps digging into my shoulders. I'm damp with sweat and my arm's aching. I fan gnats away from my face and listen to the continuous whine of my bike. I start imagining Joey's voice in my head. I talk to him. I beg him to wake up and tell me what happened. I beg him to be okay. I want to be at the hospital, to know exactly what's going on, but I have to do this first. Maybe I can find a clue, something that will help.

To the stream of cars that pass, I figure I look like a confident cyclist who knows where he's heading and where he'll end up. But I don't have a clue. I can do the grunt work, but Joey's the one who has vision.

I pass strip malls along both sides of the highway, and asphalt parking lots filled with cars. I sniff the air and smell exhaust. The cloud of french-fry odor hanging over the road by the strip of fast-food restaurants makes my empty stomach growl. I wish I'd eaten something at my place before heading to Joey's. When I'm training I eat a lot of spaghetti and cereal to keep my energy up.

I cross a major intersection. If I went left, I'd end up at Alicia's house, which is on the other side of the woods behind Joey's. The signs of the town soon disappear, and the smooth pavement of the four-lane avenue narrows into a rocky road. It reminds me of the roads we took on the second day of our spring break bike trip, when we felt fresh again after our night in the cabin.

We headed east that day, deeper into Georgia. Every road was either under construction or newly paved so we had to go slow. Early on we got behind a house trailer pulled by a white truck flashing a yellow light. We couldn't go around it because the road was curvy, and we couldn't see what was coming. We couldn't pass it on the right because there was no shoulder to ride on. Traffic slowed to a near standstill.

Joey started singing, "We're stuck behind a trailer with tornado clouds ahead. I hope we get to moving soon before the tornado comes and blows away my head." He sang that song until the truck pulling the trailer turned.

Soon after, we got stuck behind a truck hauling chickens in wire baskets. Feathers floated past us. Joey pulled around the truck and passed. I followed. When we were in front of the chicken truck, he said, "I think that calls for a song," and he sang "Circle of Life," which reminded me of *The Lion King*. We loved that movie when we were little.

A couple of miles later we came to a fried chicken place.

Joey said he couldn't help it, he was craving fried chicken. We pulled in, bought a bucket of chicken, and went into a wooded area, where we saw two armadillos playing. They ran away. I was thankful Joey didn't sing as we ate.

When we arrived at the place on the map where we planned to spend the night, the campground wasn't there. Farther down the road we stopped at a dollar store to buy bottled water and more baby ointment. Joey got into a conversation with the cashier and before long the cashier invited us to sleep in his front yard.

We set up the tent and sat outside. The stars were so bright they seemed close enough to fly to. By the light of the porch Joey worked out the details for our cross-country trip. He mapped out the route along the southern part of the country right through my hometown, Endurance. I want to visit the hospital in Endurance because the staff always sends me a birthday card, and I like looking around in hospitals, comparing how they run things. Joey said a lot of hospitals send birthday cards, and he knew because he'd got one from a hospital in Atlanta every single year.

"And I thought I was special," I said, grinning.

The next day we stopped at a bike shop and poked around. It was like being in a toy store. I looked at everything. I wrote down prices. I chewed my lip. I did the math. I didn't have enough money to go. I think I'd always known I didn't, but it was easy enough to forget when Joey and I fantasized about the trip.

"Maybe my bike can make it," I said unconvincingly.

"No way, man." Joey looked over the new bike. "You need a

touring bike. A real one like this. You don't want it to break down in the middle of podunk Kansas."

I ran my hand over the seat of the bike I'd like to have. It would last me a long time if I took care of it. "I can't go," I told Joey. "I want to, but I can't." I said I didn't have enough money. He nodded and looked away. We walked outside. The sun was so bright my eyes burned.

"We don't have to sleep in motels at all," he said.

"Think about air-conditioning, showers, clean sheets, and television. You wanna go without any of that for a month?"

"We don't have to eat in restaurants," he said. "Ever."

"Now, that's just crazy," I said. "I want to have fun along the way. I'm not looking to suffer, even if it's supposed to be a survival challenge."

We pushed our bikes down the sidewalk and stood under a dogwood in full bloom. "So what are you going to do? How did you think this would happen?" He didn't sound angry, just disappointed, like a father or something.

I shrugged. "I don't know."

"I'll loan you money."

I shook my head.

We crossed the street. "When *will* you be able to go?" he asked.

"I'll be ready when you finish spring quarter at Duke. Every book I've read advises against going during the summer anyway."

"Man, I thought we were really doing this." He kicked at the gravel, sending up a cloud of dust.

"We will."

He didn't say anything else. He was too nice to make me feel bad. But I still felt like shit.

We left our bikes outside, went into a log-cabin restaurant, and sat in a booth by the window. We both ordered catfish. While we waited and looked out the window, Joey came up with the idea of my moving into the shed and living rent-free. I wouldn't even have to buy food. I could help out around the house while he was at Duke, in exchange for room and board. He figured I'd save a lot of money. "Then you can also go to the community college, make good grades, and transfer to Duke in a couple of years."

I looked around the restaurant. Just about every table was taken. I overheard the manager asking a customer if he'd go up the hill to Donna Faye's house and ask her if she could come to work.

"Don't count on the good grades and transferring to Duke plan," I said. "I'm not moving into the shed."

"Okay. There are other ways," he said, getting excited. "There's financial aid to help pay for college. You can get a job and loans. Colleges love poor students with pretty good stats."

"Colleges love students who can pay full price and have great stats, and I'm not one of them."

"But you could try," Joey said. "It'd be the supreme challenge. There is nobody like you."

Lucky for everybody else.

The manager came over to our table and asked questions about our trip. He'd noticed our bikes outside and the way we were dressed. He gave us free dessert and said to come back again. We nodded like we would. When we went outside and got on our bikes people were staring out the windows like we were famous or something. Joey and I waved back like we were.

We rode 150 miles the second and third day of our trip, making a total of 234 miles.

Monday, 2 PM

Joey's house sits off the road across from a sprawling cornfield. Thick woods surround the property. Even the area we burned up when we were learning to camp is a thicket of weeds and young trees. All the vegetation looks dull and exhausted from the heat and drought.

The gravel on the Chanceys' driveway crunches under my bike wheels. The drapes are closed and both of their cars are gone. Joey's Kia is in the driveway, though. I can almost imagine that I'll walk into the shed and see him sitting there. I stand frozen in Joey's front yard, where I don't belong anymore, wishing I could start Saturday over. I could've helped him somehow. I would've gone to the party and taken care of him if I'd known about it. I cup my hands around my mouth. "Champ!" I yell.

I don't see him anywhere. Usually he'll wiggle from underneath the front porch and run to me barking and wagging.

I roll my bike to the backyard and hide it behind a pecan tree. A metal trash can sits next to the barbecue grill. I go over and look inside. Somebody's been burning trash. I pull on a burnt plastic bag that resembles the white bag with the yellow tie that I keep in the shed. I see my other cycling shorts, a rain jacket, and pants, all charred.

"Damn it!" I shout. Mr. Chancey has always had a temper,

and he was quicker to unleash it on me than on Joey whenever we got into trouble together. He must really think I got Joey drunk. Hasn't anyone told him I was at work when it happened? Doesn't he realize I'm the last person who would want to hurt his son?

I pick through my stuff. It's all ruined. That gear cost me at least an entire week's pay. My scorched cycling magazines are here too. I pull the bag out and look into the bottom of the can. There's broken glass and a condom wrapper. Where did that come from? Who was Joey hooking up with?

Michelle.

I kick the trash can over and over.

CHAPTER 11

Two Months Ago

That bike trip during spring break was kind of like my relationship with Michelle. The whole time I was with her, I wondered how we would ever make it another mile. Sometimes things she'd say would make me feel like the dog I hit with my bike—temporarily stunned. The thing is, she never cared about me as much as I cared about her. I don't think she could really care about anyone but herself. I figured that out when I started getting to know her from the inside out.

One night I was scheduled for 11 PM to 7 AM, and before work I met up with Michelle in the courtyard of the funeral home. My first mistake was mentioning that I wasn't in the mood to work, and my second was saying that a few friends were at the Watering Hole.

"Don't go to work," she said. "I mean, it isn't like the place will fall apart without you." She handed me her cell phone. I said no, I couldn't call in sick. To make her happy, I said we could go to the bar for an hour or so, before my shift started. I threw my bike in the trunk of her car and she drove.

We found Joey at a booth in the back. Alicia and Wade were at the bar ordering nonalcoholic drinks, which the bar served on Sunday nights for the high school crowd. Guys always brought flasks with them anyway.

I went to get drinks. I heard Alicia and Wade already arguing because he was staring at Michelle and panting like a dog. Alicia hit him on the shoulder.

I got our drinks and went back to the table, where Joey and Michelle were talking intensely. I set a drink in front of Michelle. She was leaning toward Joey with her back to me. Joey was saying he planned to take physics, Chinese, differential calculus, and chemistry his first semester at Duke. I just sat there and waited for her to turn around. Finally I said, "Here's your drink," kind of loudly. "How nice," Michelle said. She started talking about college with Joey and telling him where to buy extra-long sheets for the dorm beds. I was kind of annoyed, but mostly I was jealous. Eventually Joey asked me how work was going, and we talked about that.

For a while I forgot about going to work. I arrived an hour late and had to lie about getting bumped by a car on my bike.

I met up with Michelle outside the funeral home the next evening. She was waiting on what she calls the veranda in the front. I would've called it a porch. It was about a hundred degrees out. She jumped up from a rocking chair, wrapped her arms around me, and kissed my cheek. I grinned. How could I be this lucky?

"I wondered if you'd be waiting," I said. "I'm glad you are." I took her hand and we walked to the garden across from the funeral home.

"How could I not be? It's like I've known you forever."

We sat on the stone bench. "It's like eighth grade was yesterday," I said.

She giggled. "I wish it were. I'd wait after class for you."

"You wouldn't. You were shy then." I was shyer.

She smiled. "I'd let you do my homework."

I laughed. "You'd fail."

"If you did my homework, it wouldn't matter."

"Why?" I said.

"Because I'd know you really liked me."

I got warm all over. "Want to go to a party? It's in a few weeks, but I need to let Wade know as soon as possible. He wants to rent a house on the lake for the weekend."

"I don't know. It sounds great. Is Joey going?"

"Probably. We do just about everything together."

"You have his number?"

"Why?" I asked. I liked that she got along well with Joey. At school, I always hated not feeling like a part of a group. Now I felt like I was.

"To ask him about the party, silly. Did he remember me from eighth grade?"

"I didn't ask him. I didn't see any point in talking about eighth grade. I'd like to wipe middle school from my mind."

"Me too," she said. "And my boarding school. Everybody there thought they were entitled. Everybody thought they belonged at the top." She pushed her hair behind her ears, and it reminded me of the ponytail she wore back in junior high. "Why don't you ask Joey if we can all ride together?"

"Sure." I wouldn't mind standing at a party in a group with Michelle on one side of me and Joey on the other.

Michelle was looking at her fingernails. I heard a chattering noise. A gray squirrel sat in the fork of a tree chewing on a pinecone. I was thinking about what to say next.

"Want to go to a movie tomorrow?" Michelle said at last, running her thumb across her fingernails.

"We could go in the afternoon," I said. "I have to work later."

"I hate going in the afternoon. I'll ask somebody else."

My throat closed up. I gnawed on the inside of my mouth. Is she going to ask Joey? I wondered. The squirrel dropped the chewed-up pinecone onto the gravel. For a while all I thought about was who else she was going out with. I wasn't about to say anything. When you're feeling lucky to have a girlfriend like her, you don't want to mess it up.

A week later I asked Joey if Michelle and I could get a ride with him to Wade's party. We were in Ridge Pharmacy, where Joey worked, and he was pulling expired laxatives from the shelf. You wouldn't think something like that would expire. You'd think the older it got, the better it would work.

"Sure," Joey said. "I already told Michelle it wasn't a problem."

I was pretending to be a customer, picking bottles off the shelf and looking at them. "You talked to her?" I asked. I'd never given Michelle his phone number.

"I ran into her the other night at a movie."

"Funny," I said. "She mentioned asking somebody to a movie since I couldn't go."

"A bunch of us were there." Joey was reading the label on a blue bottle. "I'm surprised you'd shell out the money for Wade's party."

"Why?" I asked.

"You hardly ever go to parties. You hardly ever want to talk to anybody. You need to talk instead of just standing around."

"Nobody talks to me. I don't know what to say. I don't have anything in common with them."

"You must really like Michelle to spend all this time and money," he said in a bitter voice, and laughed. "You don't even have time to train anymore, and you keep canceling our weekend bike trips."

"It's not her," I say. "I work most of the time."

"Oh yeah? I called you a couple of times at work. You weren't there."

"Probably because my hours keep changing." I set down a bottle of stool softener I was pretending to inspect. "Why don't you like her?" I said.

Joey looked down the aisle and turned toward me. "She's all right. But Wade's going to want to get into her pants."

I was speechless for a moment. I wasn't expecting that. "I don't think he'll fit."

Joey crouched and looked at the bottom shelf. "I was just kidding around," he said. "But I am worried. You go to work late, you call in sick, and you never have any money when we go out."

"I'm going to pay you back," I said.

I saw the pharmacist-owner headed our way. "Do you need some help?" he asked.

I didn't want to get Joey into trouble. I shook my head. "My grandmother told me to pick up a laxative," I mumbled. "But there are too many to choose from."

Next thing I knew I was buying some fiber supplement the pharmacist recommended and Joey was ringing it up.

One Month Ago

Before Wade's party, I had my nails manicured by Andy's mom, who worked at the Beauty Palace. I'd gone in for a haircut and mentioned I had important plans. She suggested a complimentary manicure. She said nobody would notice the clear polish. I guess she figured I needed all the help I could get.

I changed my clothes three times and used styling gel on my hair. When I stood in front of the mirror, I looked right. Not like some loser. My dad even said I looked nice, but he was frowning. I'd called in sick for both that Saturday and Sunday. I felt crummy about that.

Mr. Chancey gave Joey and me this advice right before the party: Use a lot of sunscreen, wear gloves to dig, and space the azaleas three feet apart. Joey had told his parents we were doing volunteer work for the botanical gardens and he was spending the night with me.

We picked up Michelle. I got out of the car to meet her at the door and then she got in the front seat. I had to sit in the back, which felt kind of weird, but I tried to forget about it. We took a two-lane highway to the lake and after about a dozen turns we found the house on an isolated road. Wade's father had rented it from Saturday morning until Sunday afternoon for six thousand dollars, but half of that was a damage deposit. Each of the sixty guests had to pay a hundred dollars. That included food, drinks, and a booze cruise on the lake. I paid for Michelle and myself, which left me with $6.40 in my bank account. You do stuff like that when you're either insanely happy or stupid. Michelle had brought along a large bag, and I kidded her, saying I was sure the place already had a kitchen sink.

We parked on the road and got out. Because of all the trees in the front yard, all I could see were the brick steps and boarded-up windows on the second floor. It looked like one of those haunted houses in a movie where you just know a serial killer is hiding out.

Michelle waited until Joey and I were out of the car and then changed from baggy jeans and an old-lady blouse into shorts and a tight T-shirt. Her stomach showed a belly-button ring and a tattoo of a baby python.

Joey stared at her belly like he'd never seen one before. I took Michelle's hand. "Maybe we'll leave in a while," I said, suddenly nervous. Every guy was going to be checking her out. I was also thinking I should go to work the next day instead of staying off sick again.

"Oh no," Michelle said. "We can't leave early. I screwed up. I told a friend about the party. He might pop in with a couple of friends, but I'm not sure when. I hope you aren't mad." She was talking to Joey.

Joey glanced at me uncomfortably. I shook my head. I'd never told her she could invite somebody—especially a guy. Wade wasn't going to like having his party crashed. He'd make me pay the extra, and if I couldn't, I knew he'd ask Joey.

We stepped into an entryway. A large box had a sign taped above it—LEAVE UNDERWEAR HERE OR JUST LEAVE. My stomach tightened.

"I brought a change of clothes," Michelle said. She pulled a bra and panties from her bag and held them up for us.

Joey's mouth dropped open. I snatched the underwear and stuck it back into her bag. "That's crap," I said. "It's just one of Wade's jokes." I looked into the box. It was almost full.

The main room was shabby and crowded, the air dense with smoke and noise. A nasty-looking orange couch sat in the middle, and some guy I didn't recognize had already passed out on it. Oily stains spotted the plywood floor, and the blinds on the three windows facing the front yard were shut. Static-filled hard rock blared from a stereo. I didn't know many people, but I knew that a lot of them weren't wearing their underwear anymore.

Joey pushed his way through the crowded room, and Michelle grabbed his hand to keep up. I straggled along a few feet behind them like an obedient puppy.

I came up behind Joey and Michelle and stood on the outside of the group. "The booze cruise is canceled," Wade was saying. "My dad says he's not going to be responsible for a bunch of drunk kids in a boat on the lake."

I tapped Michelle's shoulder. "I'll get drinks. What do you want?"

She shrugged. "Whatever."

I walked away. I found the kitchen and poured myself some ginger ale from a bottle on the counter into a red plastic cup. That way, nobody would see what I was drinking. I couldn't get drunk if I was going to work tomorrow. There were three people

100

at the table, but they didn't look over at me or say hello or anything. I poured Michelle a cup of wine.

I went back to the great room. I didn't see Michelle or Joey. Wade was next to the bathroom chugging a beer. He finished and let out a long burp. "That's disgusting," Alicia said.

"Sexy, you mean," Wade answered, grinning his stupid smile at another girl.

This was not how I'd imagined it. I sat on the floor next to the stereo. I pulled a CD from the bottom shelf. *Aerobic Yoga*, the case read.

I'd only been out with one girl besides Michelle. Her name was Estella, and I took her to the homecoming game. She didn't speak much English, and I didn't speak anything but English, but she was the niece of the head of housekeeping at the hospital, who had talked me into the idea. I learned some Spanish. I learned *Me duele la cabeza. Quiero a mi casa* meant *I have a headache. I want to go home.* Estella said it a few times and got one of her friends to translate it to English.

I walked around some more. I went upstairs. A bunch of people were trailing into one room. A puff of smoke escaped as the door slammed behind them. It sounded like there was another party going on in there. I twisted the knob. The door was locked. I knocked. Somebody opened it a crack. "I'm looking for Michelle," I said.

"She's not here," the guy said, and closed the door in my face. Obviously I'd found the stoner room.

I went outside. It was dark, but in the light on the pier I could see Wade, Alicia, and Joey standing with about ten other people. I took a deep breath and told myself to go down there and join the crowd. Everybody was horsing around, taking turns throwing each other into the black water. No way would I do that, but I figured they'd leave me alone. When I got to the pier, Alicia grabbed me and started pulling me toward the edge of the water. I yelled, "Don't! Don't!" I couldn't tell her why throwing me into the water was a bad idea. They'd make fun of me forever. Wade picked me up like I was a rag doll and tossed me into the water. It was cold, and it was deep, and I don't know how to swim. Nobody noticed my failure to surface. I thought I'd at least have a chance to float to the top and wave for help. Instead I was sinking. I started to panic, thrashing my arms, which only seemed to send me down faster. Next thing I knew Joey was in the water. He pulled me to the surface and onto the dock. I lay on my back shivering like a scared Chihuahua.

"He should've said he couldn't swim," Wade said in a slurred voice. I heard a round of laughter.

I sat up. I figured I looked less stupid upright. Most of the others were heading off someplace else. Even drowning I'm boring.

"Why in the hell didn't you tell them you couldn't swim?" Joey said, teeth rattling. "You act like anything somebody does is all right because you think they're better than you." He locked his arms in front of his chest.

"I wasn't drowning. I was just about to get out," I told him.

Michelle came up behind us. She had a smile on her face like I'd never seen before. She said, "You are amazing." She wasn't talking to me.

Joey shrugged and plopped on the dock next to me with his legs hanging in the water. When he didn't say anything back to her she said she'd get some towels and headed off.

"Where you been?" he asked me.

"Walking around. Seeing what everybody else was doing."

"Figures," he mumbled.

Lake water dripped off my nose. "I talked to a few people."

"Michelle's friends showed up. You better tell Wade you didn't know anything about it. When he finds out he'll ask you for more money. I'll kill you if you pay him anything."

I looked out over the water and focused on lights in the distance. "I will," I said. "But I don't think you need to tell me what to do all the time."

"I'm just looking out for you," he said. "I'll mind my own business from now on."

I squeezed water out of the hem of my shirt. Michelle came back with a towel and Joey and I took opposite ends of it. Michelle sat next to me. I sneezed, and you'd have thought it was the funniest thing in the world. We laughed, and I didn't even wonder why Michelle got up and moved between Joey and me. They were doing all the talking anyway, so I guessed it was easier with her in the middle. I looked up at the moon. I could see its monkey face staring at me.

CHAPTER 12

Monday, 2:14 PM

I get my backpack from my bike and plod across the grassy yard toward the shed. My toes hurt. If you don't want your toes to hurt, don't kick a garbage can across a backyard.

I lick salty sweat from my lips and open the door. I wonder where Champ is. It hits me that I'm a lot like the stuck puppy Champ once was. Always just kind of hanging and trying to become a part of the world, not sure what's going on.

Joey and I always sleep in the shed when I spend the night. I've spent lots of nights, sometimes a few in a row, but I always had to go home sooner or later. Sometimes I slept here when nobody knew it except Joey. My school records list the apartment as my home, but I practically grew up in Joey's backyard, the shed, and the woods.

I smell pine. Looks like somebody's been busy cleaning. The

room is in perfect order, and the broken window has been duct-taped. Joey must be doing all right, since Mr. or Mrs. Chancey took the time to burn some of my things and clean the shed. I figured the Chanceys would be keeping vigil at the hospital. I turn on the radio. I don't like the quiet.

A flash of memory hits me. Joey naked and swinging a hoe, the overturned table, the glass.

But I don't think the party was in here. It wasn't wrecked enough, it's too small, and Joey's parents could've come home unexpectedly.

"Hey, it's your ol' friend Dr. Dobie. Keep your dial on WBZI for the best in classic rock music. It's a scorching ninety-eight degrees in the shade, but I've got good news, folks. There's a front moving in from the west and looks like we'll have rain by late Thursday or early Friday."

I get Champ's dog food and fill his dish. Then I fill his water bowl. I set both of them outside the door. I'm going to miss that dog if Mr. Chancey says I can't come over anymore.

I go over to the traveling backpacks and lift mine off the hook. I look inside, and I can tell nothing's missing. Maybe he didn't burn this because he didn't know which one was mine and which one was Joey's.

I survey our gear. Even if the trip's been postponed a year, Joey said we should keep collecting what we need. He's got a list with twenty million items on it. The odd thing is, we've been packing since we were twelve but there's always more to add.

The only thing missing is the garbage bag with my clothes for the trip, the cycling magazines, and my books. What kind of a man burns books?

I move over to the crate and open the side filled with my stuff. I see the football Dad gave me when I turned six. Joey and I used to practice with it until I quit the football team to work at the hospital. One of the reasons I'm so good at kicking trash cans is my experience as the field goal kicker.

The other side of the crate contains stuff Joey and I played with as kids. I see GI Joe with the missing head, Superman, Batman, and the folders of comic strips Joey and I wrote and drew for the school newspaper. My favorite comic strip was the last one we made. It was about these two superheroes who were stranded in space after being hit by a meteor. The engines of their spaceship were damaged and the radio was broken. They were on the outside of the ship trying to repair it, but being superheroes, they were better at supernatural feats of heroism than actually fixing anything real.

We got bored with it when we couldn't come up with a good ending. We left them drifting in space.

From the highway a car whines. The sound grows fainter and fainter until it dies.

I won't take anything that belongs to both of us.

Now that I'm packed, I have to look around. I hurry to the storage area. I'm looking for drugs. I don't know what kind, but because Joey was hallucinating before I found him and pushed him, it has to be drugs. I find tools, work gloves, fertilizer, weed killer, tomato food, insecticide, fishing equipment, and a lot of junk. I take only a couple of minutes to pick through it all and then run to the back of the house. I try to lift Joey's window. Somebody's locked it.

I use my fake American Express card to open the kitchen door. It's one of those with *your name here* engraved on the bottom. I covered that part and carried the card in my wallet to impress Michelle.

I rush to Joey's room. If I hear a car I can get out his window without a problem and make it into the woods. I've done that enough times to be an expert.

The night of Wade's party at the lake, Michelle got puking drunk. She was going around kissing just about anybody so Joey and I brought her back here. We climbed through Joey's window so we could use his private bathroom. Then we went back to the shed, and Michelle undressed in front of us, down to her bra. She passed out on the bottom bunk bed. I felt embarrassed, seeing her like that with Joey standing next to me. The next morning we had to sneak her out so his parents wouldn't see.

Joey's room is neat but still smells like Champ. I figure Joey's parents and the police have already searched his room for alcohol or drugs or whatever. I go straight to the hidden panel beneath the waterbed. I lie on my belly, open the small door, and reach inside. When we were younger, Joey hid porno magazines here. All I find are cobwebs.

I sit on the bed. A framed picture of the two of us on graduation night sits on his nightstand. Next to it I see our senior year yearbook, with *Harvest* embossed on the cover. I reach over and open it to the page displaying the baby pictures of the graduating class. One picture has my name beneath it, but the baby is really Joey. He's wearing a blue T-shirt that reads SPECIAL DELIVERY. I'd never had a baby picture taken. "In fifty years," Joey said on the day we got our yearbooks, "we can look at the picture no matter where we are and have a good laugh."

I start reading his autographs.

You are awesome, bro. I'm going to vote for you for president.

You're the smartest guy I know.

You are so sweet and cute. You should be cloned.

I know I was probably really annoying always bumming help off you.

I have thoroughly enjoyed having you in my class. You are an inspiration . . . Mr. Stray had written a whole page to him. I'm not surprised. Mr. Stray, our biology teacher, once told Joey he was destined to do something great. After that Joey would talk about finding a cure for cancer or developing nanotechnology to use inside our bodies.

I'm feeling guilty reading all this stuff, but I can't help turning to the last page and reading the small words written in the top right-hand corner.

DON'T FORGET ME. THANKS FOR EVERYTHING.
YOU'RE MY BEST FRIEND.

"I won't forget you," Joey said after he'd read what I wrote. We were sitting in the cafeteria. "Nothing's going to change."

I laughed. "Everything changes."

I hear the grandfather clock in the hallway strike two. I forgot I'm in a hurry. I slam the yearbook shut, crawl across his bed to his computer desk, and slide into the chair.

I'm about to check his e-mail when an instant message pops up from FelixCat.

You aren't Joey.

I quickly sign off and shut down before anybody else realizes I'm snooping using Joey's name. I don't know who FelixCat is.

My stomach growls when I pass the refrigerator. I back up and open it. They have food crammed onto every shelf. I could get lost in here. I pull out a can of whipped cream and squirt in a mouthful. Joey and I both love to eat whipped cream this way. I swallow and fill my mouth again. Whipped cream leaks from my mouth. I swallow, lick my lips, and decide to eat properly, like I appreciate the food. I get two slices of bread, spread on the whipped cream, and take a bite. Crumbs fall out of my mouth. I push them back in. I try to forget that I've snuck into Joey's house and am stealing food.

I don't think. I chew slowly. The whipped cream is cool and sweet, the bread stale.

For the past eight years, Darcy, Dad, and I have spent every Thanksgiving with the Chanceys. On our first Thanksgiving, there were five kernels of corn on my plate. I leaned over and whispered to Joey, "Is this all we're having?" Dad nudged me with his elbow.

Joey said that it was a tradition in their family. He explained that the pilgrims had survived a harsh winter. As a reminder to be thankful for their blessings and the plentiful harvest, they placed a few corn kernels on their plates.

Mr. Chancey said the blessing, and then everybody had to say what they were thankful for. I was thankful to eat, because with all the tradition stuff I was near starved. Joey said he was thankful for his parents, his dog, and me.

After that, Dad started our family tradition. At Christmas, we always have noodles. Long ago he told Darcy and me that when we moved out, he wanted us to always have noodles on Christmas because we had survived on them the first year we were here.

Monday, 2:45 PM

Outside, it's all clear. The road's as deserted as the cornfield across the street.

"Champ!" I shout, looking under the front porch. "Come on out, fella."

In the slivers of light between the porch slats, I see Champ's tennis ball and an old teddy bear he likes to sleep with when he isn't in the shed.

I slide out from under the porch. Champ's never run off anywhere, but he likes to chase trucks. I laughed the time he chased a UPS truck down the highway and Joey took off after him wearing only his boxers.

Maybe Joey's fine now. Maybe he woke up and when I get to the hospital he'll be apologizing to his parents for his mistake, telling them he'll never get drunk or take drugs again. Telling them I had nothing to do with it.

A bird flutters into a tree. Insects buzz and gnats get in my eyes. I hate it when gnats get confused and go up my nose.

The party could have been in the woods behind the house. Joey's parents and the police wouldn't know that kids hang out back there. Champ loves to go back there and chase squirrels or go swimming. So I might find Champ as well as evidence of the party. I follow the dirt path behind the pecan tree where I've left my bike and head toward the creek. I hear the birds sing and see a blue jay sitting on a branch of a red maple tree. After about a tenth of a mile I pass the short path leading to the pet cemetery. Joey and I used to have funerals for his pets. We'd bring Kool-Aid and pick flowers and carve miniature tombstones from Ivory soap. Champ's mom, Goldie, is there, along with a turtle, a snake, a cat, and a betta fish, but the tombstones never endured the weather. They'd melt like snow into the graves. I stop and yell for Champ.

After half a mile I come to a fork. If I go to the left, I'll end up on a gravelly path leading to a road fenced off with chicken wire. There's a beat-up sign that reads TRESSPASSERS WILL BE SHOT. .

I take the path to the right. Trees and shrubbery choked by kudzu close in on me from both sides of the path. A shadowy tunnel of green. After another tenth of a mile, I'm at the creek. Mosquitoes stick to me and suck my blood.

I'm scared to look in the water. You never know what you'll find floating. A few bubbles pop through the green scum on the surface. Cigarette butts are scattered among beer cans, bottles, potato chip bags, condom wrappers, and big red plastic cups. Somebody left a sock on the wild blackberry bush.

This is where the party was, but I'm sure Joey wasn't the one who gave it. He never liked to give parties, just show up at them and be able to leave whenever he wanted. Then again, I thought he'd never try drugs, and it seems pretty certain now that he did.

I cup my hands around my mouth and face the creek. "Champ!" I yell. "Come here, you son of a bitch!"

I put my hands on my hips and look around. You can't cross the creek here unless you can jump at least eighteen feet and the bank isn't slippery with mud. Joey and I pushed a fallen pine tree across it once, but it's rotten now and the wood pops and cracks if you step on it. Past here, the vegetation is thicker, but you can eventually get to Alicia's subdivision.

She'd have a party in the woods. Heck, she'd have a party on a highway if she thought she wouldn't get run over.

There are only minnows and tadpoles in the creek. No rabbits or deer or rats roaming today. Once a wild pig chased Joey and me, but we jumped the creek. The pig got bored and went the other way.

I used to think it was beautiful and magical out here, but now it's only the place where something happened to Joey. I take a deep breath, smell the decay, and tell myself not to worry.

One afternoon in the eighth grade, Joey called me and said to meet him by the creek. It was an emergency. I jumped on my bike and pedaled to Joey's. Then I sprinted through the woods.

Joey was sitting by the creek. I went over, sat down, and asked him what the trouble was. He said he had something good and something bad to tell me. So I just listened. He'd gone to a birthday party the night before and made out with a drunk girl.

I sat there and gawked at him.

"The next thing I know she was rubbing me, and there were all these other kids around doing even more than we were. I figured what the heck. Then we went into the bathroom and hid behind the shower curtain."

"Oh my God," I said. "You did it in the bathtub?"

Joey grinned. "We did everything but that," he said. "She wanted to, but I couldn't."

I let out a whistle. "That is bad news," I said.

"That's the good part," he said. "I wouldn't do it with some-body drunk. Then she got sick and threw up so I just left her there."

"So was that the bad part?" I asked.

"I woke up this morning and found out I caught something."

"Like what? A cold?"

"I have a venereal disease." He wouldn't look at me.

"What? You're shitting me." I started to laugh.

"Shut up," he said, red-faced. "It isn't funny."

I held in the laugh. "I don't think you'd have symptoms of some disease right away, and I'm pretty sure you have to do the deed."

"No," he said. "You can get it from oral sex, but I don't have that kind. I mean, I have pubic lice."

I exploded with laughter, but not before I jumped up and ran.

He came after me. "Want to see?" he yelled. "Want me to share?" I took a flying leap over the creek, missed, and landed in the water.

I crawled out of the water. "Don't come any closer," I said, dripping. "Or I won't tell you what to do."

He stayed by the blueberry bush.

"Nobody has to know. There's this special shampoo you get at the drugstore."

Monday, 3:55 PM

I need to hurry. I have to be at work in three hours, and I have to check on Joey. I sit on a log. I stare at the water. The girl Joey fooled around with that time back in eighth grade, the girl who gave him crabs . . . she was Michelle. He told me a few days ago. All those times the three of us hung out together and they never said anything.

CHAPTER 13

Monday, 6 PM

I arrive at work an hour early, but I don't clock in yet. I need to talk to the Chanceys. After I left the creek I went back to my apartment to empty my backpack. My dad was home. I told him Champ was missing. He nodded but kept his eyes on the television. I didn't stay long.

After I shower and change, I'm feeling rejuvenated, although my face is stinging from sunburn. It's Monday so the emergency department probably won't be as busy, but I hope to spend most of the night helping out down there. The energy takes my mind off things.

I go to the ICU waiting room. I can't screw this up. Talk to them the way you always have, I tell myself. Don't say anything about your things getting burned. Maybe they thought it was a bag of garbage.

I walk into the waiting room hoping that Joey has his tubes out by now and is talking. "Hello, Mr. Chancey, Mrs. Chancey. How's Joey?"

Joey's father sits staring at me without moving a muscle. Cold air from an air-conditioning vent in the ceiling circles around me. Mrs. Chancey stops pouring a cup of coffee. I remember how the mother comforted the kid in the ER the other night so I go over and give her a one-arm, chest-to-shoulder hug. I never really hug anybody.

I can smell coffee on her breath. I can feel her stiffen. Oh boy. Was I ever wrong when I was hoping they wouldn't still be mad at me. I move away.

"You should have told us you pushed Joey," she says quietly. "The police told us today."

I look past her ear toward the exit. "I pushed Joey but I didn't mean to hurt him," I say. "I was going to tell you."

Mr. Chancey suddenly comes alive. "Where you been, Clay? Didn't you get my message? Are you afraid of me?"

His loud words could wake a cadaver. I hope nobody in the hall can hear him. I take a deep breath. "I went to feed Champ. I couldn't find him," I say, shaking.

Mr. Chancey looks at me like somebody inspecting a tub of worms, and from the expression on his face, I think I'm the dirt. He's probably thinking up the best way to kill me. I stand up straight with my head high. Mr. Chancey hates it when Joey slouches. "So you and Joey were fighting," he says.

The cool air is wet with the smell of Mr. Chancey's aftershave. I squirm like a cut-up worm. "Joey came after me," I say. "I pushed him away."

"Why?" he says.

"Why?" I repeat, a hundred heartbeats more scared.

He grunts. "Usually a person doesn't attack another person without a reason."

"Didn't you talk to the doctor? Didn't he tell you Joey was confused and fighting?"

"You didn't have to push him to the ground." Mr. Chancey rises from the chair. I don't think he's looking to shake my hand. "You have no discipline. You've always run wild, and you've always made Joey take stupid chances with you. Like these bike trips. And the partying."

Mrs. Chancey wears an expression like the one she had the day she found a snake lying on the toaster.

"I was trying to help him. I didn't even know about a party," I say.

Mr. Chancey sits and covers his face with his hands. He sighs hard. "Right, you don't know anything." He looks up and glares at me. "You know, Clay, in a lot of ways you're just like your father."

"Clarence," Mrs. Chancey whispers. "Let him alone."

"Do I look like I want him here? Aren't you supposed to be working instead of bothering families?"

I stare at the floor, at his ugly black shoes. "I'll check in with you later."

I hurry out of the waiting room and lean next to the pay phone. I breathe slow and deep to calm down my racing heart. He talks to me like I'm nothing. Like I don't have feelings. He bought me a new bike when I turned ten, and the Schwinn bike I ride now when I turned fifteen. He picked me up when I got sick at school as a kid. And now he's burned some of my clothes. Nothing will ever be the same again. Nothing.

Mrs. Chancey walks out of the waiting room.

I turn toward her. "I'm sorry," I say, but she grabs my arm gently before I can walk away.

Every year on my birthday she makes me a cake and sings "Happy Birthday." Dad and Darcy never did that.

Mrs. Chancey's eyes are red around the edges. It hurts me to look at her. I glance down at the lines between the tiles on the shiny floor. I figure if I got on my hands and knees and looked close, they'd have dirt inside them.

"Do you want me to get you something to eat?" I ask.

"No," she says. "And I don't want you visiting Joey. I don't care who started the fight. All I know is that he's lying strapped down and on a ventilator, and you're standing here breathing. Do I make myself clear? We love you, Clay, but right now we need to look out for our son."

"Yes," I say. "Okay." She hates me because I breathe.

Monday, 6:50 PM

Mrs. Hunt gives me orders to wash a bed. Somebody from the housekeeping department has already mopped and cleaned the room, wiping down all the surfaces with an antibacterial solution, but they didn't finish the job because the shift ended. I put a hospital gown on over my scrubs and then pull on gloves. I'm careful not to get the solution on my skin. According to the package insert, it causes skin irritation in rats.

There's nothing like bed washing to get you in a mindless mood. All I have to do is move my arms. I don't need my brain. I don't have to think.

I try to do a good job. One time Ms. Hunt saw a room I'd

cleaned and said I did the best job of anyone. I've seen her pitch a fit when she finds a room not adequately cleaned. I've heard her say that germs in a hospital kill.

I lift the rails. I start at the headboard, spraying it carefully with the disinfectant. I wipe in one direction. Then I do the side rails and footboard. I put down the rails and do the mattress. Most people would probably call my work mundane. I see it as important.

"Hey, Clay, you busy?" Charlie asks from the doorway. He's a couple of years older than me and has worked here a lot longer than I have. He's a Med Tech 2, and he's studying premed. He also helped transport Joey to CT Sunday afternoon. Charlie doesn't wash beds or mop floors anymore, and he knows everything that goes on in the hospital. You'd think he'd be smart enough to see I'm occupied. I know he's about to ask me to do something he doesn't want to do.

"Yeah, Charlie. I'm doing heart surgery on the invisible man." The mattress is dry now, so I flip it over. It slams onto the bed frame.

"You having a bad night?"

Awful's more like it. "Nah. It's just peachy. Can't you tell?" I start wiping down the other side of the mattress. Charlie leaves and comes back a few minutes later with linen.

He starts helping me make the bed so I know he's about to ask me to do some of his work.

"You know Chief Baker?" he asks.

"Yeah."

"He wants to see you as soon as possible. What'd you do to him?"

I look up in surprise. "What are you talking about?"

"He was admitted with chest pain this morning."

Shit. Chief Baker is the one person who believes me. "He had a heart attack?" I ask.

"No, but he's having some tests, and he's pissed off at you."

I shrug. "He can get in line behind everybody else who's pissed at me."

Charlie tucks the sheet under the foot of the bed and makes a perfect corner. "Can you shave him since you have to go into his room anyway? Don't let him scare you. His tough-guy routine is just an act."

I throw on the blanket. "You're just saying that to get me to do your work."

"No. Really, he's all right. He stopped me for speeding once. He told me if I ever got into trouble again he'd take my liver out and stomp on it. But he didn't give me a ticket." Charlie slips the cover on the disposable pillow. The pillow is covered with a plastic wrap. I take it from him, pull off the case, and put the pillow on the bed with the case on top of the pillow. This way, whoever admits a patient to this room has to remove the plastic wrap first, and they won't forget to remove the small yellow tag, which is how we keep track of supply charges.

"So will you do it for me, since he wants to see you anyway?" Charlie says. "I've got to help take a body to the morgue. I guess you could do that instead."

That convinces me. "I'll shave him."

"You sure you can handle it?" Charlie says.

My head's nodding.

Charlie pulls out a wadded piece of paper and hands it to me. "Here's the room number and instructions," he says, and waves as he heads out of the room.

"Wait."

Charlie stops. "Shit. I should've known you'd want payback."

"Can you get me the results of Joey Chancey's CT?"

"I already know. He has an acute subdural hematoma."

I look down at the white blanket. I bet it matches my face. I don't want to believe that Joey has blood on his brain from an injury. Acute means it happened recently.

I can't move. I can barely breathe. I didn't push Joey that hard. "Nothing showed up on the first CT," I say.

Charlie shrugs. "A subdural hematoma doesn't always show up right away. I knew a man who didn't have any symptoms until two weeks after his injury. All that time, he walked around dumb and happy."

"Do you think Joey's going to be okay?" I ask.

"Joey was stable after his craniotomy."

Craniotomy? Jesus. A doctor opened his skull to remove the blood.

I lift a side rail, and the lock clangs shut. I start to spray the cleaning solution. I keep spraying. Charlie puts his hand on mine. "You've done that already," he says. I look and see the rail so wet it drools like a sick old man. Then it hits me. I don't know what I'm doing, and I've got to get my shit together before I make a big mistake.

CHAPTER 14

Monday, 7:30 PM

As I walk down the hall to Chief Baker's room, I'm glad I have something to occupy my mind so I don't have to think about Joey and his brain injury. I'll focus on shaving. I've been trained to do that, although I've never shaved anybody but myself before. I'm more nervous because the chief of police wants to talk to me.

Mr. Chancey showed Joey and me how to shave when we were twelve. As he lathered his face with shaving cream from Belgium, he said, "Do you boys know about sex and disease?"

My nose stung from the smell. I looked over at the bathtub with its little feet and started wondering why somebody would build feet on something that couldn't run away.

Joey quickly suppressed his grin. "No, Dad. We don't know anything."

But we did. We'd learned it in health class, and from talking about it, and from watching channel ninety-nine. Even scrambled, it was pretty informative.

I thought it was strange that Joey was so eager to listen to his dad when we could've been doing something interesting.

I rotate my bruised shoulder. It seems like everything I do has a way of reminding me of Joey.

I glance into Chief Baker's room. He's staring at the TV. His face looks more wrinkled now. On his bedside table sits a pamphlet with a heart on it.

He's going to kill me.

I take a few deep breaths, knock, and enter. "How you doing? I hear you're having a sex-change operation."

He doesn't answer. He's watching *Cops*.

Maybe I went too far. "I'm here to shave you," I say, like I'm an expert. "Can you hear me?"

He turns his head from the program and rubs his whiskers. I don't know why he can't shave himself. "I'm not deaf. This is all your fault. I don't need anything but to go home." He pushes back the half dozen or so gray hairs on his head. "I can't even take a shower or go to the bathroom by myself. I'm afraid I'll be electrocuted."

I've never seen a scared cop before.

I keep myself from laughing. "I see what you mean," I say as I untangle the monitor cord from around his neck. "You've got enough wire here for the electric chair."

He scoots up in bed. "A lot you know."

I shrug. "But you can't be electrocuted," I say. "Somebody caught on fire once, but they were smoking in bed."

I can't believe it, but he's laughing. I check his arm tag and the bed label and ask him his name.

He stops laughing. He loses the smile. "God, Clay. You know who I am." His eyes are wider than the foam electrode, and he has goose bumps on his arms.

"We're supposed to always check identification," I explain. "So we don't screw up. I wouldn't want to accidentally shave the lady in the next room."

"Son," he says. "You have big problems if you don't notice the difference."

I open his drawer. "Where's your electric razor?"

"You think I had a chance to go home and pack first?" he says. "I thought I'd be here for an hour, and instead they admitted me for a bunch of tests."

I slide toward the door. "Be right back." I head down the hall to the supply room and get a razor and shaving cream. I stick the little charge stickers on my scrubs to put on his green card. Sometimes I go home with yellow stickers all over me. I need to work on that. I get yelled at for lost charges. Farther down the hall I get a washcloth and towel from the linen cart. I go back to his room. I need one of those little gadgets to measure how far I walk at work.

After I fill his brand-new disposable washbasin from his admission kit, I lather his tissue-thin skin with shaving cream. I drag the razor in a long, smooth stroke over his bristles. All he does is look at me sort of helplessly. Not too long ago he was asking me questions like I was guilty of something, and now I have a razor on his neck. I hope I don't cut him.

At the oxygen tubing, I stop, lift it, and shave. I rinse the razor and swipe his square chin, bypassing the fat mole with the single hair.

He asks about my family. I put down the razor, take my wallet out, and show him a photo of Darcy dressed as an elf in tenth grade. "Pretty girl," he says. "Nice smile."

"Yeah," I say. Darcy always made sure my teeth were taken care of. When I was a kid, she'd make me brush my teeth while she sang, "Brush, brush, brush your teeth," to the tune of "Row, Row, Row Your Boat." Sometimes I still catch myself humming it when I brush.

I show him a picture of my mother, my father, and Darcy when she was a baby. "That's my whole family," I say.

"Where are you?" he says.

I shut the wallet quick. I'm wasting time. "Unborn." It would be impossible for my mother and me to be in the same picture. "So, did you have a heart attack?" I say.

"No, I did not have a heart attack," he mocks in a high-pitched voice.

"What are you in for, then?" Mrs. Hunt is constantly lecturing me for saying inappropriate things to patients. Like when I told a patient once he should get another doctor's opinion. Seems more like common sense to me than something inappropriate.

But Mrs. Hunt's cool. She can't bear to lose a patient, and when she does she always tries to go to the funeral. She sends the family a plant if she can't make it. I figure it's a good substitute.

"I'm having an angiogram," he says. "To see if I have any blockage in my heart arteries." The blood pressure cuff on his arm inflates. When I look over at the monitor, it reads 190/110. "You know anything about that test?"

"No, sir. I never read the pamphlet. I guess you didn't either."

"The doctor is going to run a tube into my heart from my groin," Chief Baker says. "And you said I wouldn't be here long."

I know sometimes when they do that test, they go ahead and clean out the arteries if it's needed. I think it's kind of like unplugging a stopped-up toilet. I'm not going to tell him that.

"But I never said I was a doctor," I say. I concentrate on what I'm doing so I don't get nervous about cutting him. I'm a little shaky, the room is hot, and I'm wondering if Chief Baker can smell my sweat when I lean in close to him.

The day Mr. Chancey taught Joey and me to shave, he turned to me afterward and said, "Clay, you stink."

"What?"

"You smell. You need to wash better. And do you use deodorant?"

"Yes," I mumbled. I turned and ran. Joey was in his room so I hid in the shed and cried. I was so embarrassed. Nobody ever knew I was out there crying.

"I'll have to lie flat for a few hours after my test. I won't get out of here until late tomorrow at the earliest. My cat is home alone. She's probably scared and hungry." I hear the monitor above his bed. His heart skips a beat.

He looks at me, and I feel like I have a stamp on my forehead that reads CAT FEEDER.

"You owe me," he says. "You talked me into this."

"Owe you? For getting you some much-needed medical attention?" I sigh. "Why ask me? You don't even know me."

"I know where to find you," he says. "And it's easier to keep up with you this way."

I get to wondering how somebody as smart and powerful as a police chief who probably knows everybody in the county could end up without a single soul to see about his cat.

"I'm working all night."

"The morning will be soon enough."

"Where's your key?" I ask.

"In the nightstand." He tells me his address and directions. He lives in an older neighborhood a few blocks from the hospital. "Just feed Pumpkin and scoop out her litter box."

"I don't scoop. Want me to call so Pumpkin can hear your voice?" I add sarcastically.

"I don't need to talk to my cat on the phone."

I finish off his face and dry it with a towel so rough it could take off skin if you rubbed too hard. I don't see any cuts.

Chief Baker opens his over-bed table and glances into the mirror. He smiles and rubs his hand over his face. "I feel better, son. Look better too."

He doesn't look that much better, but the blood pressure monitor reads 140/80. After I clean up after myself, I walk out of the room whistling, and I don't ever whistle.

Monday, 9 PM

I go to the third floor to empty catheter bags and record the amounts of urine. When I get to Mrs. Parker's room, her door's shut tight. I ease it open and slip inside. The room's dark and she appears to be asleep. She told me once she hates to have her door shut because she likes to watch people go by. I don't know why patients tell me stuff like that. I never ask questions, but I always listen when they start talking. I don't remember anybody ever coming to visit Mrs. Parker.

I go into her bathroom and get the clear plastic container used to measure her output. I squat at her bedside looking for the bag of urine that should be there. I can't find it. I move to the other side but it's not there, either. I stand and notice she's dead. A sheet covers her body, and part of her foot is sticking out with the toe tag showing.

The last time I talked to Mrs. Parker she gave me a banana. I guess I looked hungry.

She was terminal. I'd seen the NO CODE sticker on her chart. She knew she was dying, and she didn't want anybody trying to save her. I wonder if anybody ever asked her to not give up. Mrs. Parker was thirty-nine.

I go into the hall and close the door. Mrs. Hunt walks over like she's been waiting for me. She's not smiling. "Clay," she says. "Did you prep Baker?"

"I shaved him."

"You didn't follow the instructions on the sheet. You were supposed to shave his groin."

"Sorry. I didn't realize—I haven't been trained to shave any-thing but a face," I say, thankful I have an excuse.

"You've been trained to read instructions. You should have come to me and I would have showed you how to prep a patient. I shaved him myself. The next time you make a mistake, you'll be written up." She turns, stops, and glances at me over her shoulder. "Whatever you did or said to him helped. He's calmed down a lot, and his blood pressure has improved." Mrs. Hunt adds, "Remember to stand up straight, Clay, like you have some pride."

I wheel a new patient to his room, mop up some blood in the emergency room, and walk a patient down the hall and back because he's supposed to do that three times a day. Then I talk to the respiratory therapist for a while and watch closely as she suctions an emphysema patient on life support. I thank her for showing me, and she smiles and says I can observe her anytime.

There's a kid on pediatrics who won't go to sleep so I play Barbie dolls with her for a while. Her name's Holly. In a few hours she's getting transferred to a children's hospital, where she'll get chemo. When I go, I tell her I enjoyed playing Barbie dolls and wish her good luck. She waves goodbye.

The rest of the night I help turn patients, change beds, and empty urine from more catheter bags. By the time my shift ends, I feel like I've walked a thousand miles down every hall in this hospital except the one in the basement that leads to the morgue and the one that leads to Joey's unit. I'm scared his parents will see me and have me fired. But maybe I'm more scared I'll find out Joey isn't doing any better.

Tuesday, 7:05 AM

After I clock out, I sneak into the ICU and stand out of sight by a fire extinguisher. At the nurses' desk, Dr. Sermons, a neurosurgeon, is talking to a nurse. I'm pretty sure she's Joey's doctor. She's the only female neurosurgeon I've ever met. She can save him if anybody can. Well, not counting God, but I figure Mr. Chancey's already tried that route.

I pick up a stack of sheets from the linen cart and start

walking. I peek into the window of Joey's ICU room. Mr. Chancey's holding Joey's hand. Mrs. Chancey's rubbing Joey's feet. His blood pressure is 124/76, his heart rate is 74, and his oxygen level is 99 percent. Those aren't bad readings for someone in a coma. At least they have him stabilized, and often a coma is just a temporary state while the body heals itself. Joey's repairing himself. He'll probably come out of this stronger than he was before.

I see Mrs. Chancey say something to her husband, and they both stare at Joey's face. Even with the tube in his mouth, Joey looks peaceful. Kind of like he's gone someplace inside his mind where he's safe and content and somebody like me isn't spying on him behind a stack of sheets.

CHAPTER 15

Tuesday, 7:10 AM

I pedal toward Chief Baker's house, wishing I hadn't messed up the plans for the cross-country trip, that I'd had the money to go ahead with it. Joey and I would be nearing the end of the journey now. Instead of being in the hospital, Joey would have been camping out under desert skies.

It feels good to be out in the air, but I can barely make my legs move, I'm so tired. I'm hungry, too. I should've stopped by the hospital cafeteria for coffee and the Tuesday-morning Belgian waffle special.

I turn my bike onto Bloom Street and look for Chief Baker's house number. I wonder what Michelle's doing right now. I wonder if she's thinking about me. I bite my lip. I don't want to think about her not thinking about me.

But I can't turn off my brain.

About two weeks ago Michelle showed up at the shed close to tears. It was kind of late at night, and I didn't remember telling her I'd be there. I figured she had been looking for me. She walked in with a couple of bottles of wine, sat at the table, and pulled out a joint. Joey told her no smoking in the shed and no wine. He couldn't risk it. If his dad ever found out, he'd be in big trouble. She smiled at him sweetly. He rolled his eyes.

She told us her parents had been yelling at her all day for no reason. She had no friends because of them, and her mom had gotten pissed off because Michelle didn't want to help out at the funeral home. "They treat me like a slave," she said, "because we're short-staffed."

"I guess nobody's dying to work there," Joey said with a grin.

It was Joey's idea to play this stupid game where you have to smash eggs against your forehead not knowing if they're boiled or raw. Joey's mom had made potato salad for dinner so we had a few boiled eggs. Michelle went wild during the game and hit Joey in the face with a raw egg. Then she pinned him down and licked his face. At the time, I laughed and howled like a wolf. Joey pushed her off after a few seconds. "You're going to get salmonella poisoning," he told her as he went to the sink to wash his face. Then he said he was going into the house because he had an egg-ache.

I followed Joey to the door, and he told me she couldn't stay all night and to make sure she wasn't seen by his mom or dad. I knew about their rules. I always obeyed.

Michelle picked up the bottles of wine from the table and said she had to go.

"Already?" I asked. "I was hoping we could spend time together without anybody around. Just us."

"Oh my God. You're jealous!"

I kind of laughed. "I wouldn't mind if you licked egg off me."

"I got carried away," she said as she opened the door to go. "It didn't mean anything."

It meant something. I suspected that then and I know it now. I go around a pothole and focus on the house numbers. I shut out a deserted feeling that's coming over me. The houses in Mr. Baker's neighborhood are old and in need of repair. His yard looks like a forgotten cemetery. I'm thinking I'll ask him if I can do some yard work. I wouldn't mind making extra money.

I get off my bike and push it onto his porch.

The inside of the house smells like a litter box. A fat tabby cat on the faded blue couch hisses at me. Her fur stands straight up on her back. I touch her gently. "Hiya, Pumpkin. My name is Clay, and I'm not scooping out your litter box."

She purrs and moves her back up and down against my palm. Her collar jingles. "I like your necklace. It matches your fur."

I've got this habit. I don't talk much to people. I talk to animals.

Pumpkin obviously spent the night playing Tarzan. Broken lamps and dirt and leaves from an upside-down plant cover the gray carpet. The curtains on the sliding glass door are halfway off the rod. Pictures from the fireplace mantel lie on the floor. A piano dominates the far corner of the room. An elaborate cobweb stretches between two of the legs.

In the kitchen I search for cat food. A torn package of ground beef sits souring on the counter. I guess Pumpkin didn't care for the smelly meat. Champ's not like that. When he finds something rotten, he rolls in it. I toss the meat into the garbage can.

Champ. I wonder if he's come home.

Chief Baker's cabinets are filled with boxes of macaroni and cheese. You'd think somebody like him, with a stable job and a real house and all that, would have something in his cabinets besides pasta. When we first moved from Texas, we lived off noodles for months. Buttered noodles. Ketchup noodles. Mustard noodles. Mayonnaise noodles. And for dessert, syrup and noodles. That was my idea.

I look into the refrigerator, sniff and swirl the milk. Chunks float to the top. I ignore the beer and take a Coke from a six-pack. On top of the refrigerator, I find crackers and cat food. I empty Pumpkin's cat food into a bowl that reads CAT IN CHARGE. I place it on the coffee table, then sit on the sofa and eat with her.

When Pumpkin's finished eating, she climbs into my lap, turns in circles, and lies down. She smells fishy. I rub her ears and she purrs and stretches. "I guess I should leave," I say, but I'm sure she wants me to stay. I wish I had a place like this myself. I'd fix it up a lot nicer.

I walk through the house looking around. Some people might call it snooping. I call it snooping. Pumpkin follows.

Crystal wine goblets and plates thick with dust line the shelves of the china cabinet in the dining room. Cat-paw tracks trail across the table. Upstairs most of the doors are shut. I open each one and look inside. The rooms are clean but dusty and the air is stale. One small room contains an unmade twin bed and a shelf crowded with golf trophies and pictures of Chief Baker, his wife, and a bunch of kids. I wonder why he sleeps in here when he could choose one of the bigger rooms.

Pumpkin jumps on the bed and meows like she's hurt. "No

wonder you went nuts," I tell her, rubbing her ears. "Being alone in a crypt."

Pumpkin purrs.

"Here's the deal, cat. I have to get going now. Have a nice nine lives." I'm trying to close the front door when Pumpkin sticks her head in the way, meowing loudly. I glance down at her. She looks way too sad for me to go off and leave her alone. "You sure are friendly, considering you just met me," I say. "I suppose I can hang out here a little while, since you're lonely." I go back inside, locking the door behind me.

I start thinking how pathetic it is that Chief Baker didn't have anybody to feed his cat and how desperate he must be to trust me, of all people. I think Joey is the only other person who trusts me, but the two of them couldn't be more different.

Joey had this assignment for language arts in the middle of our senior year. He had to write a story or essay based on the best thing anybody ever said to him. I didn't have to write one. I wasn't in AP.

"So what's the best thing anybody's ever said to you?" Joey asked. We were in Joey's room. He was at the computer. I was sitting on the bed. "It can't be 'I love you' or anything like that."

" 'I trust you,' " I said. "You said that to me before I took that fishhook out of your eyelid. Or you could use what your letter from Duke said about how great your essay was."

"I haven't been accepted yet, though," he said. "Besides, it isn't that great. Going to college hundreds of miles away, meeting wild college girls, going to parties on the weekend, classes all day, studying at night. Not knowing a single person, competing with people who are smarter than me who probably play every sport there is. Kids from big cities who can find their way around.

Kids who've been to Europe and all over the world. You don't know how good you have it."

I shifted on the bed. It was funny in a way. Joey wasn't scared about biking across the country, but he was afraid of rejection, going to college, and growing up. He had all this amazing stuff on the horizon and he only talked about the negatives. Maybe he just downplayed it all for my sake.

"Give me a line," Joey said.

"How about 'You're my best friend, Joey.' I said that."

"I know." He looked down like he was embarrassed.

So Joey wrote this story about a kid who showed up at his house on Christmas Eve half frozen to death, and he was shy and scared of everything and didn't have a single friend in the world. The kid became his best friend. They spit into a bottle and became blood brothers. After that they did everything together. When they were older they started planning and training for a cross-country bike trip. Joey's story was published in the school's literary magazine. It was a good story, but I hope that wasn't my fifteen minutes of fame.

CHAPTER 16

Tuesday, 12:15 PM

I open my eyes and stare at the ceiling, confused. Shit. I hope I'm not where I think I am. Then I feel Pumpkin asleep on my head. I remember lying down on the couch for a power nap, but by the light coming in through the windows I can tell it's past noon already. I wipe my face with my arm and groan. Chief Baker probably wouldn't be so happy about some strange kid crashing on his couch while he's in the hospital. I guess he never needs to find out. It's not like Pumpkin can talk, unless she's seriously holding back on me.

The cool air is filled with cat smell, but it's not bad. The couch is soft and smooth like an expensive T-shirt. I turn on my side, cuddling against the back cushions.

I'm doomed to live in a tiny apartment with my dad forever. I'll never be able to afford to move out. He's been in a ten-year rut—ever since the building where he worked burned and we moved from Texas. All he does is work at the same measly hourly rate, eat, sleep, and gain weight. He wants to find somebody like my mother, and once in a while he goes to a bar with his garbageman buddies, searching. He doesn't drink, he just sits around at the bar staring, probably scaring every available woman off before they're even close enough for him to say hello. At least that's how I imagine him. Sometimes he gets teary-eyed and says how much he loved my mom. He'll say he wishes he could forget. I think he has posttraumatic stress disorder, because of my mom dying and the factory burning. I learned about that from a psychologist while I was helping him transport a psychotic patient who was strapped to the bed.

I wonder if Dad's noticed I haven't been home since yesterday. Last time I talked to him was Sunday evening—almost two days ago.

Pumpkin moves right up to my face. I stretch and spit out fur. I have to go.

Tuesday, 12:50 PM

I walk into my apartment and turn off the air conditioner. My dad keeps it cold in here. Most people wouldn't think about that, but I do. My part of the electric bill runs around a hundred dollars a month, which is more than half of a week's pay. I need to work more.

I'm feeling lousy so I call Darcy as I lie down on the couch and watch the ceiling. She's always good for a laugh.

"What's wrong?" she says immediately. "You sound tired."

"I worked all night and haven't had much sleep. I have to be back by three to work the evening shift."

She tells me she didn't make it to the audition yesterday. Her voice sounds tired.

"What kind of audition was it?" I ask.

"To sing in a club. I didn't really want it anyway. How's Joey?"

"He had a craniotomy because of a subdural hematoma."

"What?"

"Joey bled into his brain," I say. My voice is trembling. "So they operated."

"Wait a minute. What does drinking too much have to do with bleeding into your brain?"

"It's called blunt-force trauma."

"Cut the jargon, Clay," she says. "What's going on?"

"His alcohol level showed he was drunk. His CT of the brain showed a clot from receiving a head injury."

"The head injury you gave him?"

"Well, yeah, I pushed him, in self-defense."

"What do the doctors say?"

"I don't talk to them. They won't tell me anything anyway."

"What do Mr. and Mrs. Chancey say?"

"They're mad." My hand's sweaty around the phone. "Mr. Chancey burned some of my things," I say.

"The Chanceys are angry because they're in a lot of pain, and mad people can be unreasonable. I don't even want to imagine what it's like for them," she says, and I notice how her voice has changed. "Why don't you come up here and stay for a while?"

"You mean run away."

"You could end up getting the blame for this."

"That won't happen."

"Oh yeah? What about the innocent people spending years in prison because some witness lied or made a mistake or an arrest is needed in a case? A lot you think you know. You don't know anything."

"That's in murder cases," I say. "This isn't like that."

"If he dies it will be felony murder."

I'm getting sick to my stomach. "Joey isn't going to die. And I think I know what happened."

I tell her there was a party in the woods, and somebody must have given Joey something—I'm not sure what. That's why he was hallucinating before I arrived. I tell her Michelle got stoned in the embalming room and came on to me when I tried to question her about it.

Darcy laughs. "I'm sorry," she says. "But that's just weird."

"Yeah, especially after she had said it was over with us. She also said Joey was better than me. She said Joey wanted to be with her."

"And you believe her?"

"I don't know. It doesn't matter now." I try to say it like I mean it.

"Vic's done that to me." She goes on to tell me about the last time she was here. She went to a business dinner with Vic. He barely spoke to her or introduced her to anybody. It was like she didn't measure up. She went back to Nashville and forgot Vic.

After I hang up, I close my eyes. I figure you get one best friend in your life. You'd even die for him if you had to. Well, maybe not. But you're so close to him you become his shadow.

Sometimes you have arguments, but they're mostly about small stuff. Then you meet a girl you care about. The first time she meets your friend you get knots in your stomach. You feel almost positive that she'll care more about him than she does about you because everybody else does. But things are okay after they meet—she still cares about you, and she likes your friend, too. You think you all have grown close, but when you notice her looking at him, you feel left out, and you wonder. How could anybody not love him the most?

Then one day you learn the truth, and a day later your friend is in the hospital on life support.

Four Days Ago

As Joey's stashing the fishing rods in the trunk of his Kia, I come out the front door and see Michelle pull up in her Corvette. Something makes me stop in the door frame and watch. Maybe it's because she always seems to be asking about Joey. Maybe it's because she's wearing a halter top and Daisy Dukes.

"What are you doing here?" he says.

"Do you want to hang out?" she asks.

"Clay and I are going fishing."

She looks toward the porch. I don't think she sees me. She turns away and says something.

"You can't just come over here whenever you feel like it," Joey says loudly.

"Call me later." She gets back into her car and pulls away.

I set the cooler on the porch, walk down the steps, and get on my bike. "Did Michelle just stop by? Why didn't you get me?" I try to sound casual.

Joey steps in front of me. "I'm only nice to her because of you."

"Or maybe because you want to be with her."

Joey laughs. "Right. She's a poor little rich girl who thinks she's entitled to anything she wants. You deserve the Golden Asshole award, Clay."

"So not only am I stupid, but only some trashy girl wanting to use me could possibly like me, right?"

He looks more annoyed than sorry. "Listen, she's the girl I hooked up with in eighth grade. The girl who gave me crabs. She's been coming on to me. She always has. You've seen her."

I stand frozen for a few seconds, astonished. "Thanks for waiting two months to tell me," I finally say. I start biking away.

He yells my name. He chases after me. I ride down the highway.

I have a stranger buy me a twelve-pack at the gas station.

I go inside my empty apartment, turn on the TV, and switch off the lights. I set the twelve-pack next to me and open a beer. The old *Body Snatchers* movie from the fifties is on. I stare.

How could they do that to me?

Joey walks in without knocking and sits on the other end of the couch. "What are you doing?" he asks, like it isn't obvious.

I shake the beer bottle. "Having a party."

"I thought so." He takes a beer from the twelve-pack between us, twists off the cap, and drinks. "This is a great movie," he says.

I nod. "Yep. The main characters wonder if their friends and family are real or if they've been replaced by pods. The pod people don't have any emotions." I sip the bitter beer.

"Lots of small-town paranoia," Joey says. "That's how it was during that era."

"I don't think it's that irrational. Aliens could exist."

"I guess so." Joey props his legs on the coffee table.

"Have you done it with her?" On the screen a giant pod pulsates ominously.

"No."

I turn off the TV. "I wish I believed you."

He shakes his head. "I'm tired of you acting like an idiot."

I shrug.

Joey convinces me to go to the Watering Hole with him. He pulls his car into the parking lot of the bar. Michelle's sitting on the hood of a car in the parking lot, and this guy I've never seen before is standing between her legs. She doesn't see us.

"How did you know she would be here?"

"She called me after you left today. She asked me to meet her here, said she was feeling pent-up and needed a release. I said no. I wouldn't do that to you. She laughed and said she wasn't giving up. She told me to tell you to leave her alone."

"Fuck you," I say. Joey did this to me on purpose.

He starts to say something but I jump out of the car and start walking home. Nobody comes after me. Not Joey. Not Michelle. Nobody.

CHAPTER 17

Tuesday, 5:05 PM

Chief Baker's been moved to a regular room where he isn't hooked up to all kinds of wires. He waves at me with the newspaper. His dinner tray sits untouched on the bedside table. "How'd the test go?" I ask from the end of his bed.

"When they injected the dye I thought I was on fire. But I don't have to lie flat any longer." He sets the newspaper on the bed.

I take a deep breath. The meat loaf on his tray smells great. I'm trying to remember when I last ate some real food. I suck in my stomach. Sometimes if you press your belly in, you can trick it into not feeling empty. Unless you smell food. But I don't really mind being hungry. In a weird way it actually helps me concentrate. "So what's wrong with you?" I ask.

"Nothing. The doctor said my coronary arteries were so

clean we could have a picnic inside them. I told the doctor all along I had indigestion, not heart problems," he says. "I guess I proved him wrong."

I shrug. "All you had to do was lie there," I say. "You didn't prove anything. You never know when you might fall over dead from something that could've been fixed."

"I had the test, didn't I? I still have a lot of miles to go before I die." Chief Baker puffs out his chest a little but he doesn't look that strong to me. "How was that damn cat?"

I stare at his food. "She's just terrific. She pulled down your drapes, broke a lamp, and turned over a plant. But it was dead anyway. Want me to go back later? I get off at eleven."

"I'll be discharged soon," he says.

I'm kind of sorry I won't get to go back to his house. "Aren't you going to eat your roll?"

"No. Is something bothering you, Clay?"

"Why are you asking?"

"Because you have circles under your eyes, and you act like you're starving."

I tear open the roll and smear on butter. "Nothing's wrong. I just forgot I was this hungry." If Mrs. Hunt walked in right now, I'd get fired for eating off a patient's tray.

Chief Baker opens the drawer of his bedside table, takes a twenty from his wallet, and says, "I almost forgot. This is for feeding my cat."

"That's okay," I say. I stuff a bite of the roll into my mouth.

I watch the bill disappear as Chief Baker returns his wallet to the drawer. He could've insisted. I ask him if he ever thought about hiring somebody to do yard work.

"Let me think about it." Chief Baker watches me. "I've asked around about you," he says. "You're a hard worker, and I like how you take responsibility. You have a lot of integrity." He turns his head toward the window. "You must be feeling desperate."

I try to smile. "Why? I just hate to see good food wasted." Actually, I hate to see his bad food wasted.

"I'm worried about you."

When I look at him, it's like I've already crossed some line and there's no going back. He knows I've got nobody else to lean on right now. It's the same way with Mr. and Mrs. Chancey. In the past three days I've gone from being a part of their family to being a despised outsider.

I watch him watch me. He doesn't know I broke into Joey's house. Sucked whipped cream right from the can. I don't have integrity. I have tired legs and an emptiness inside me that has nothing to do with hunger.

Tuesday, 7:10 PM

I push a linen cart toward ICU. Before I get to the waiting room, I stop and straighten the sheets. I notice a picture on the wall of a kid sitting alone on a bridge over a river. I wonder if the artist was trying to show that the kid's thinking about jumping. He looks like it. That's a weird picture to choose for a hospital.

The waiting room is crowded, but I don't see Mr. Chancey. The people stop talking, stop drinking coffee, and look at me like they think I've arrived with some kind of news. It's funny how people treat you differently when you're wearing scrubs and have a stethoscope around your neck. Mrs. Chancey motions to me from the couch. I look up and down the hall. Mr. Chancey's nowhere around. I take a deep breath and smile.

146

I go over to Mrs. Chancey and kneel so I'm not standing over her.

"I'm sorry for the other night," she says. "I don't know what got into me."

"How's Joey?"

Mrs. Chancey stares at her lap. "He has so many tubes I don't know what's what." She looks up. Her eyes meet mine. "He may never wake up."

I put my hand on the other chair to steady myself. "The doctor said that?"

"No. I can look at Joey and know."

She can't know just by looking at Joey. She can't. "I knew a patient who was unconscious for two months. He woke up," I say. "He even remembered me when he came back to visit."

That patient was a hole in one—a gunshot wound to the head. He walked with a cane, and he talked like a drunk.

"He was doing great," I add.

Her hopeful eyes inspect my face. "Really?"

"Really."

Mrs. Chancey leans forward. "You should go now if you don't want to run into Clarence."

I stand. She's right. He burned my clothes.

"I went to see Champ yesterday," I say. "I couldn't find him."

"I haven't been home," she says.

"The shed had been cleaned up," I say. "Some of my things that were in a garbage bag were burned."

"What?" She rubs her forehead and I'm sorry I said anything about my stupid clothes. "I'm sure it was a mistake," she says.

"I hope the dogcatcher didn't get Champ," I say, but Mrs. Chancey's staring at her lap. She's stopped listening.

I need to check on Champ as soon as I can. That time I hid in the shed because Mr. Chancey said I stank, Champ hid with me. He licked my face like he loved me.

Tuesday, 8:30 PM

I stack the last of the linen in the closet. From the corner of my eye I see the Chanceys shuffle into Joey's room. I step into the nurses' lounge and take my break, hoping I have time to visit Joey. I'm angry with him for being stupid. I'm angry with him for ruining everything. I'm angry with him because of Michelle. But I have to look into his eyes. Lift the lids one at a time and see if the pupils are big and if they change. I have to see if he's in there somewhere. The only sounds I'll hear will come from his machines, but if I get lucky I'll see a twitch of his finger or maybe even a hint of the crooked grin he gives me. We have a bond no matter what's happened. If anybody can reach him it's me.

Waiting for a chance to go into his room, I stand at the bulletin board reading announcements for in-service education. I see a letter from the organ procurement agency thanking the nurses for assisting them in the care of a patient. I turn away. I remember the patient, but I don't want to read the letter. The letters are always happy and sad, and the feelings get so mixed up inside me that I can't tell one from the other. I sag against the wall.

Stuff keeps tearing at me. The time line makes sense, but it doesn't feel real. Joey called me that morning. He went to the party in the woods during the day. He came back in the late

148

afternoon. I showed up right after work, just before dark, found the shed torn apart, and discovered Joey naked and confused. I pushed him and caused a subdural hematoma.

After a while I see a nurse go into the room and the Chanceys leave, heading in the direction of the cafeteria. When the nurse leaves it's all clear in Joey's room and I slip inside. I figure I have at least ten minutes. Actually, I don't even care if Mr. Chancey finds me. Joey is more important than Mr. Chancey.

I don't remember ever seeing so many tubes or wires in any patient. Saline with potassium chloride hangs above his bed dripping slowly down a plastic tube, through an IV machine that counts the drops, and into a plastic triple lumen catheter in his neck. The heart monitor beeps fast but steady. He has the oral endotracheal tube and is connected to the ventilator. There's a nasogastric tube in his nose. A bag filled with urine hangs at the bedside. Joey's face has swelled. His head is wrapped in a turban-like bandage, and a tube sticks out of his skull, leading to another monitor at his bedside that measures the pressure inside his head.

I swallow hard. He looks like a monster from some science-fiction movie. I walk to his bedside. I've never been great at starting a conversation with a person who won't be able to talk back. The feelings inside are like a frozen drink from a gas station.

I guess I could say, You deserve this. You did this to yourself.

I guess I could say, Please be okay. Or maybe, You're the one lying there, but you should know that I'm hurting for you. That you're not alone.

I keep my mouth shut. I pull up one eyelid and then the other. I can't tell anything. I thought I'd see some kind of spark, but his eyes are glassy and blank.

A couple of nurses laugh somewhere outside the door. Maybe one of them told a joke. Joey always likes a joke. We've played a lot of them on each other.

I find a piece of paper and a clipboard and sit at his bedside. "Joey, you have to try," I say quietly. I start sketching a picture and labeling it so Mrs. Chancey will understand what the tubes are for. I can see why most people would be scared to death when they see Joey. I'm scared too, but drawing the picture makes me feel better.

I close my eyes and set my hand on his bed. I can't touch his arm yet. I tell myself a story in my head.

You're thirteen years old, and the two of you are in the woods. You didn't make the basketball team. He's trying to say it doesn't mean anything. He says that because he made the team. You walk away. You go deep into the woods to the creek, where there are snakes. You're convinced you've seen an alligator in the water once, but it was just a floating log. You freeze as you feel something moving on the back of your neck. You hear him trying not to laugh. You realize he's got a long stick and he's running it across your neck. You jump up. He runs. You run. He stumbles into a clearing with neck-high weeds and then his face distorts. He waves his arms madly before he falls over. You panic. You go after him. He's on the ground, and his face has an ugly look. "Snakebite," he can barely whisper. You don't think. You act. You pick him up and somehow get him across your back, and you run. After a minute your lungs are ready to explode and your legs are burning. "Faster," he cries in a strangled voice. "I'm almost dead."

You drop him. He's laughing. You forgive him because he thought of a good joke, and he grins at you like you're special. He says he never knew anybody could run that fast carrying somebody. A month later he convinces you to go out for football. You make the team. You're the star . . . until you have to quit when you're sixteen. You see that your dad's having trouble paying the bills, and you're broke all the time. You need to get a job. "You were even better than Wade," Joey says the day you quit. "You could have been great."

Tuesday, 8:40 PM

I leave the paper with my sketch on his bedside table and stand. "You're going to be okay, Joey, and when you wake up, we'll talk about what a shithead you are." I get a couple of pillows and prop him on his side facing the window. "You can see the sunlight in the morning," I say. "Or maybe the pigeons. They like the window ledges. Can you imagine how much pigeon crap somebody would step into if they wanted to jump?" I laugh for Joey. "You gotta try to make yourself wake up, because each day it's going to get harder, see? You have to keep fighting. I know you're in there somewhere."

I untangle some of his tubes. It takes a few minutes. Me untangling something, making sense of a mess. That's a laugh.

I can't get rid of my anger. It's there underneath my sadness and my fear. When I picture Michelle and Joey together, I can't stand it. I shut my eyes. I can almost feel Joey's weight on my back that day as I was running through the woods, how his fore-arm squeezed into my neck, how I didn't care about how hard I was breathing and how much I was sweating. All I wanted was to get him somewhere safe.

At the nurses' station I ask Jan if Joey's on some medicine to keep him knocked out. She shakes her head.

"Has he been responding any?" I ask.

"No. Hopefully we'll see some blinking soon. Maybe some turning of the head."

The head. It sounds so alien.

"And then what?" I ask.

"That means he's starting to wake up."

"When will that happen?"

She shrugs.

In the hallway I glance into the waiting room. Everybody's gone except for Mr. Chancey. I guess he didn't see me in Joey's room. Maybe he doesn't care anymore. He's sitting hunched for-ward like the pretzel man at the circus Joey and I went to when we were nine or ten. We rode an elephant that day as Joey told me about a circus tent that had burned to the ground with everybody inside. He mapped out our escape.

Mr. Chancey's lips are moving and his hands are clasped to-gether. I know he's praying but it looks more like begging. Tears are running down his face.

I step next to the pay phone, wait for the insides of my eyes to stop vibrating, and wish the hate inside me would go away. Mr. Chancey's scared. What I want to do is go into the waiting room and talk to him. But I can't stand up straight or look him in the eye. He'd punch me out. He burned my stuff.

I clock out at a few minutes past 11 PM, but I'm not in the

mood to go to my apartment, and I have to start work at 7 AM. I call my dad from the pay phone in the lobby and ask him to check on Champ tomorrow. He grunts okay. I almost ask him to pick me up but I stop myself. He'll fall back asleep and forget. Besides, I need to be here for Joey.

The hospital lobby's empty and cold as if everybody in the world has disappeared. I find a chair hidden by a big post, sit, and read the classifieds in a newspaper somebody left behind. I circle a few apartments. I pretend I'm going to rent one of them. Most of them are too far away, too expensive, too . . . I hear the invisible person on the intercom paging doctors, calling the supervisor, announcing a code.

I shudder a little. Joey wouldn't be scared to sleep in a hospital lobby. He has to be scared now, though, even if he's in a coma. I fold my arms across my chest and hang on to my shirt-sleeves. I keep telling myself, Don't give up, don't panic. Joey's told me the same thing at least fifty thousand times. If I stay calm and look at things realistically, everything is fine. Joey will be fine.

CHAPTER 18

Wednesday, 6:30 AM

I dream Joey and I are in a car going fast over a bridge. The bridge collapses. I hang on to the car door and grab his shirt-sleeve. It tears and he falls.

I wake up with a gasp and nearly fall out of my chair. I look around the waiting room, at the silent anxious faces that have accumulated here while I slept.

I've always hated biking over bridges.

I wonder what the Wednesday-morning breakfast special is in the cafeteria.

When I open the door, I smell scrambled eggs, toast, and coffee. Only a few doctors and nurses are sitting at the tables. I grab some cereal in one of those little boxes and a carton of milk. Grits are cheaper, but I can't stand the sight of them. They make me remember that bike trip with Joey. I hand my employee card to the cashier for her to scan. I hold my breath, hoping it's good for one more meal.

It reminds me of grade school, where they let you charge three meals but after that you'd have to eat peanut butter sandwiches until your parents sent in payment. I survived on peanut butter sandwiches. I love peanut butter sandwiches.

I'm working all day today, and I figure eating will give me some energy. The cashier returns my card. I find the table in the back of the cafeteria up against the wall where I always sit and sometimes sleep. I feel like I can disappear at that table, take a break from reality.

"Prove that you exist," Joey challenged me once. We were around nine years old. I breathed on him, let him feel my heartbeat. "Maybe we're not real. Maybe nothing is real," he said. "Maybe my mind created you." By the time I had to go home, I wasn't sure I existed. Not until I rolled over a rock, fell off my bike, and scraped my face on the highway. I went back to Joey's house, ran inside, and announced, "I exist because I hurt."

I finish my breakfast quickly today and start work. I spend the whole day numb, pushing Joey into the corners of my mind, until I get paged to the ICU.

Mildred, a nurse about as old as a rock, is spraying air freshener toward the ceiling in Joey's room. The room smells, and I know right away what's happened. Mildred nods at me, her silver blue hair falling out of its bun. "He soiled himself," she says in a high-pitched voice. "He needs to be cleaned up, but he has blue pads underneath so it will be easier."

I step into the room. God, Joey would freak out. Mrs. Chancey would fall apart. "I can't do this," I say flatly.

She gives me a disgusted look. "Why not?"

Then I think about some stranger seeing Joey naked and dirty like this. He'd be embarrassed.

"I meant I'll be happy to help. Is he getting any better?"

"He's not coming around. I think he's close to brain death."

I think *she's* the one full of shit. I would never say something like that when there's a chance the patient might hear. I take my assignment sheet, unfolding it slowly, my fingers trembling. I hadn't planned on cleaning shit off my best friend. And he isn't brain-dead.

But I have to do this. It's part of my job.

I'm here to work. Nothing else. Sometimes you just have to feed the cat. Get it done.

"Go ahead and give him a complete bath and change his linen," Mildred says. "Be careful and don't pull his tubes out."

Like I don't know that the tubes are Joey's connection to life.

I collect supplies: the salmon-colored basin from inside his bedside table, the motel-size bar of soap from the drawer, and his deodorant, comb, and toothpaste with toothbrush. I also get two towels, three washcloths, a bath blanket, a hospital gown, and gloves. Mrs. Hunt taught me to give a bed bath. She said, "If you don't learn anything else, you're going to learn this."

I fill a basin with warm water and test it with my elbow. I cover Joey with the bath blanket and then remove the other covers. I wet the cloth and wipe his eyes. I soap up the cloth, wash his face, neck, and ears. Then rinse and dry. Next I put a towel under his arm and wash his hand, arm, and hairy under-arm. I repeat the rinse and dry and do the other arm. His chest and stomach are washed next, followed by his feet and legs. Each time, I move the towel when I change parts.

I start singing. Not too loud. He's nothing but a body in a bed to me.

I get clean water. I roll him onto his side. Watch the tubes. They could get pulled out. They get pulled out, and he could die.

He has blue pads underneath, which are always used with comatose or incontinent patients to protect the bed. I roll them toward him. I wipe shit. I wash. I rinse and dry. I keep singing. I roll him onto the other side. I pull the pads out. I position him on his back. I wash the penis. I wash around the catheter first. Then the rest.

Mildred comes into the room. She looks at me. "Are you crying?" she asks.

I shake my head and hurry to the bathroom, sloshing the pan of dirty water.

Mildred helps me change Joey's bed. "You're amazingly thorough," she says, tightening the sheets. I'm holding Joey on his side. I'm powdering his back. I'm rubbing it in. I'm ready to roll him over and pull the clean sheet through to my side.

In two days I've had two nice things said to me. I have integrity. I'm thorough. I've set a record. "But I'm slow," I say. "I take too much time."

And I hate everybody. Even this sour nurse I don't know.

We roll Joey the other way. "You should go to nursing school, maybe medical school."

"I wish I could afford it," I say.

"Excuses," she says. "That's what everybody has when they're too lazy to try." She holds her arms out in front of her.

"See these arms?" I nod. I don't want to hear her crap. "They're the same length as yours. Probably shorter. I had to reach to get what I wanted." She opens the nightstand, pulls out something, and closes the drawer.

What the heck does somebody like her know? She doesn't understand what it's like. "I'm not lazy," I say, full of contempt. Just because somebody's poor doesn't mean they're lazy. I spray the underarms with deodorant.

She's holding up an adult diaper.

"No," I say. "No. He doesn't need a diaper—just the blue pads." My lips start trembling. My voice has cracked all the way in half. She pauses, then nods her okay. She puts the dirty blue pads into a red bag. She goes away.

I brush the teeth. I suck out the fluid with the tonsil suction tube. I stand with the machines. I breathe with the ventilator.

CHAPTER 19

Wednesday, 7:10 PM

Joey was wrong when he said our bike trip would be the ultimate survival challenge. He's already on the ultimate survival trip and I'm sitting in a chair next to his bed. I clocked out when my shift ended at 7 PM, but I don't want to leave.

Joey's lying with his eyes closed, face swollen, not moving.

This coming Friday we were supposed to leave on another bike trip to Birmingham as part of our training. It would have taken two days to cover the hundred and fifty miles.

I touch Joey's arm. It's cool and clammy.

I'll be eighteen Saturday. Before we canceled the cross-country trip, Joey and I planned to celebrate with a dinner in California. Now it'll have to be on my nineteenth birthday. We've celebrated all my birthdays together since I turned eight. Joey used to send me cards signed *Your Secret Friend*. For a couple of years I thought there was a girl somewhere with a crush on me.

Our cross-country trip will start in Savannah, at the Atlantic Ocean. We'll dip our rear tires in the water. Then we'll head toward Mobile, Alabama. When we get to the Gulf of Mexico, we'll dip our tires again.

We're going to stop in my old hometown, Endurance, Texas, and stay awhile. We'll end the trip at a small town north of San Diego. I don't remember the name. What matters is making it all the way to the Pacific and touching the water.

"I'm getting a touring bike soon, to start breaking it in," I tell Joey. I stand and smooth out the wrinkles in the pillow behind his back. "I can get a loan to buy it and have it paid off by next summer. We only have nine more months," I struggle to say. Nine months isn't so long after waiting most of our lives.

CHAPTER 20

Wednesday, 7:20 PM

I walk out of the emergency department with the Wednesday-night Lamaze class. A horn blows and I turn my head.

Chief Baker's car pulls next to the NO PARKING FIRE LANE sign, and I start shaking. "I can't do any more questions now," I say, stopping next to the car. "I'm too tired."

"Calm down. It's all right. Where are you headed?" he asks. His face is all screwed up in a frown. He doesn't look like a sick old man in a hospital bed anymore. Not like a man who'd ask somebody like me to feed his cat. He looks like a chief of police who is used to having a lot of power. He smells like the flea spray we use on Champ.

"Home," I say. "Why?"

It's hot out. I fold my arms against my chest to keep them still. Several people are heading into the emergency department,

161

followed by a few employees who know me by sight. I step back so it looks as if I'm waiting for somebody to pick me up. Joey used to pick me up from work sometimes. He'd always be waiting for me when it was raining.

"Come on. Let's take a ride."

I knew he was going to say that. He's skipped the acting nice part. If I say no, will he put handcuffs on me, read me my rights, and then arrest me for assault and battery? Wouldn't the Chanceys have to file charges for that to happen? I can't see Mr. Chancey going that far, no matter how much he hates me right now.

I look around. I don't want the other employees to see me get into a police car.

"You can put your bike in the back."

A few minutes later he's driving us down the deserted street, passing the dark buildings. I don't talk. I made it through twelve hours of hard work. I sat by Joey's bedside and talked to him. I know I can make it through this.

"You—" he starts as he parks at the police station, lit up like a fast-food restaurant.

"I know. I have the right to remain silent. I have the right to hire an attorney and all that bull."

"You aren't getting arrested."

I take a deep breath and try not to look surprised. "Okay," I say.

We get out and walk toward the entrance. "Do you ride your bike everywhere?"

I want to get this over with. He's brought me here for questioning. I wonder if somebody will be watching me through a two-way mirror.

"No," I say, suddenly feeling annoyed. "Sometimes I ride my tricycle, but the little dangly things on the handlebars fell off." I wonder if he gets a kick out of doing this to me, grilling me about Joey. I mean, he just got out of the hospital yesterday. He could wait until the weekend when I'm off work. "Aren't you supposed to be home resting or something?" I ask.

"I am resting," Chief Baker says. "And I'm looking for additional information. But I have to admit, you were clever convincing me to go to the hospital."

I shrug. "I've never been clever," I say, looking over my shoulder. "My bike won't be stolen out of the trunk, will it?"

He opens the door. "I hope not."

I see three officers inside sitting at a desk and eating pizza. Chief Baker grabs one of the boxes and keeps walking. I tag along behind.

We go to a room with a large table. I sit on one side. He's on the other. I look around for the mirror. There isn't one. I don't see a camera, either. He sets the box in front of him and then pulls a white notebook from a drawer and hands it to me. "Just a few pictures for you to look at."

Great, I get to look at a picture book while he's eating. I've almost forgotten how hungry I am until I see the cheese and the sausage and smell his pizza. Joey likes pizza with anchovies, olives, and extra cheese. When we stay in the shed, we get pizza delivered from Franco's, and we share it with Champ. He loves to rub his face in anchovies. Champ does. Not Joey.

First he shows me a school picture of a girl. She's got long blond hair and she's wearing braces. She looks around thirteen or fourteen. "Her name is Sophie," he says.

I open the notebook. The first picture—in full color—is of

an elderly lady lying in a pool of blood on a kitchen floor. The next picture is of an equally old man. He looks like he's asleep in bed, but there's about a gallon of blood on his pillow. I shut the book. "You're preaching to the choir," I say. "I see stuff like this in the emergency room, only the victims aren't dead yet."

Sometimes I see them die.

Chief Baker takes the notebook. "Their thirteen-year-old granddaughter murdered them with the help of her boyfriend after the grandmother tried to stop them from running away. Both juveniles had used PCP. They're being tried as adults."

I slouch in the chair. "Sophie is their granddaughter?"

"Yes." He takes a bite of the pizza and just sits there chewing with the notebook open. After a minute he says, "Both kids swear they didn't know what they were doing." He slides the notebook back into the drawer.

"I heard about it. That happened over a year ago." I remember that the murders were committed about thirty miles northeast of here, close to the Biggs County line. Joey and I passed through the town on the way home from our bike trip during spring break. We didn't stop or slow down. There was nothing there but a gas station. I sit straight up. "Wait a minute. PCP showed up in Joey's drug test?"

He nods.

So this is why he's so interested. He's trying to connect the dots between Joey and Sophie and her boyfriend. "I didn't give Joey PCP," I say. "And I've never heard anybody mention PCP. I don't even know what it looks like." I rest my head on my hand. "I'm a hundred percent sure Joey wouldn't take PCP or any kind of drug if he knew it. I'd bet my life on it."

"If you could do that, you'd lose your life. He did take it."

"But you can't prove he knew what he was taking. Joey will be going to Duke soon. He's in work-study. He'd know they might do a drug test, and he'd lose everything he'd worked for."

His bushy eyebrows furrow. "We're friends, aren't we?"

I bite my lip. "Somebody brought PCP to the party. Joey wouldn't do it if he had a choice."

"Did you confront him over a girl, Clay?" he asks me bluntly. "You see, I've talked to a few of your friends. Did you guys fight over her in the shed?"

I start shaking my head. "No," I say. "No. That's not what happened. We argued the day before. I went over there on Saturday to make things right with Joey. I never got the chance. You're making up a story to fit the circumstances."

"So why all of a sudden did you feel the need to make up with Joey? I mean, it sounds like he took your girlfriend."

"I saw a girl die that day," I say. "It gave me a little perspective on things."

He takes a tape recorder from the drawer and places it in front of me. "Your 911 call is a real-time recording of what happened. We can hear the yelling, the threats, and the crying."

I barely remember.

"We know you acted in self-defense, and I've seen what PCP can do to a person." He clicks on the tape, and I hear the static, the answer of the 911 operator, and a familiar voice crying and shouting. But it isn't the call I made.

He clicks off the tape before I hear anything else. "This call was placed from a pay phone nine minutes before your call. Do you recognize the voice?"

"Alicia. But I can't even understand what she's saying."

"She was so scared she couldn't even talk." I watch his big hands fold together like he's squeezing something. He's not even eating the pizza. "Was she with you?"

"Nobody was with me. I worked all day. You can check my time card." I look at my watch. Mr. and Mrs. Chancey gave it to me as a Christmas present. It has a second hand so I can take patients' pulses at work.

"I believe you, but she's not talking yet. She says she didn't make that 911 call."

"It's definitely her. I don't know how I can help you, though."

The chief lets out a long sigh and rubs his temples.

Wednesday, 8:35 PM

Chief Baker turns onto the road to my apartment complex, swings into a space, and shuts off the engine. My dad's truck is parked a couple of places over. I open the door and Chief Baker says, "You asked about doing some yard work. Are you still interested?"

I nod. "Tomorrow morning okay?"

"Sounds good." He clears his throat. "I want you to stay out of trouble."

"The PCP investigation. It's serious, isn't it?"

"You saw the pictures. We're talking about murder. The only lead I have is Joey. I need to find out where he got PCP and how many others purchased it before somebody else gets killed. You came close."

"What about Sophie and her boyfriend. They talk?"

166

"Not yet, but I'm certain that little thirteen-year-old and her boyfriend will spend the rest of their lives in prison without a chance of parole. That's a lot of years."

I can picture two kids I don't know in prison. I've heard what happens there. "Sad," I say.

"Sad? They murdered her grandmother and grandfather. Somebody Joey's age would get the death penalty—or at least the district attorney would ask for it—after he hacked you to death."

CHAPTER 21

Wednesday, Late Night

I can't sleep. I keep tossing, turning, and thinking.

When we were eleven I helped Joey build a time machine out of cardboard in the shed. "We're going into the future," Joey said as we crawled inside with a flashlight.

We ate nachos and drew pictures of aliens, flying cars, and computer-controlled houses. When we came out it was dark and the wind was howling as rain pounded the roof. The shed felt different, old, like we'd been in there for fifty years. For a couple of minutes I felt like we *had* gone into the future. "Hey, what's wrong with you?" Joey said. "You do know we fell asleep, right?"

Thursday, 7:40 AM

I zigzag down the road on my bike. It's going to be a hot day to do yard work so I decided to start early.

I wonder if Chief Baker is up yet. I grab his Thursday-morning paper from the yard, walk onto the porch, and peer into the window. The blinds are open, but all I can see is Pumpkin stretched out on the back of the couch. She turns her head toward the window and hisses. I move out of the way and over to the other window. Pumpkin leaps off the couch meowing wildly. The front door swings open.

"That's a good way to get shot," Chief Baker says. "Come on in. It'll be easier to see from the couch."

I kind of laugh. "Easier to shoot me too, I bet."

I go inside and Pumpkin darts under the coffee table. She acts like she never met me before. We go into the garage, which is off the kitchen. Chief Baker opens the garage door and the bright sunlight reveals a lawn mower and a bunch of pruning and weeding tools.

"Have you found anything out in the PCP investigation?" I ask.

"Since last night, no. But I can't talk about an investigation," he says. He rolls the lawn mower into the driveway. I tag along behind him.

"So I guess whoever supplied Sophie and her boyfriend with PCP also supplied somebody at the party?" I say.

"It's possible, but in a county with more than a hundred thousand people, who knows?" He shrugs, goes back into the garage, and comes back a moment later with a can of gasoline. He removes the gas cap on the lawn mower.

"Have you ever killed anybody by accident?"

He pours in the gasoline. "I never intend to kill anybody."

"I think Joey may die," I say. "Because of me."

"Because of a lot of reasons," he says, tightening the gas cap and standing. "Whatever happens, the district attorney won't touch the case. It's clearly self-defense. We have the 911 tape. We know Joey was on PCP, and EMTs, doctors, and nurses witnessed him hallucinating. He had to be restrained for everybody's safety."

I decide it doesn't matter. Joey's not going to die. He might be in a coma for a while, and he might need a lot of help when he finally wakes up, but I know he's not going to die. I'd feel it in my blood if he were, and today I feel okay.

After Chief Baker pulls out of the driveway, I start pruning the hedges. They're so overgrown you can't walk along the sidewalk in front of the porch without getting hit with a branch or stuck by thorns from the rosebushes on the opposite side. I cut those back too. I leave the peonies, which are in bloom with heavy pink flowers.

I carry the branches around to the back and then start mowing the yard.

My dad was home last night when Chief Baker dropped me off. He was snoring on the couch. I could hear him all over the apartment. I turned on the lights. I turned on the TV and sat in the chair. I waited. I imagined my dad waking up and asking me what's been going on or saying, "I'm glad to see you." That didn't happen. He just snored. When I was little I used to imagine myself coming home from school and Dad having a snack waiting for me. That never happened either. Mrs. Chancey always made

Joey a snack and examined every single paper in his book bag, smiling.

It's around noontime when Chief Baker pulls into the driveway. I'm running water over my face from the hose. He waves to me and tells me to sweep the sidewalk, porch, and driveway.

Fifteen minutes later I'm done and I ring his doorbell. He answers and asks me if I'm hungry. I say yes.

A Happy Meal sits on the kitchen table. "I've always collected the toys," he explains. "I carry them around to give to scared kids when I'm working on a case."

I wonder if he's deducting the cost of lunch from my pay.

I sit, unwrap the burger, and start to eat. I'm thankful when Chief Baker goes into the other room and gives me a chance to breathe. I notice how dirty my hands are so I get up, go to the kitchen sink, and wash them with liquid dish detergent.

My dirty hands remind me of something. When Joey and I were in eleventh grade I helped him with a science project. Alicia, Wade, and about ten other people participated. We swabbed our hands and then swabbed petri dishes. We allowed the bacteria to grow for several days. At the end my petri dish was covered with black bacteria and it stank worse than dirty feet. Joey and everybody else had hardly any bacterial growth, but I have a feeling they washed their hands first. At the time I felt like I had won a contest or something, but looking back, maybe they all just thought I was gross.

Four bites later I'm done with the burger. I start on the fries.

When I'm finished I go into the living room. Chief Baker is talking on the phone. I wait for him to finish talking and pay me. I look at the pictures on the mantel. They're yellowed with age.

"Those are our foster children," he says when he hangs up. "Amanda, Robin, Scot, and Juan. We adopted Juan."

"Do you ever see them?" I ask. I have a feeling he doesn't.

Chief Baker doesn't answer right away. I blow away some dust from one frame.

"Sometimes. They live far away," he says at last.

I nod. I pick up the picture. He's outside with four children. They're building a snowman.

I've only seen snow once. That was around New Year's a few years ago. Joey and I went outside. It had snowed two or three inches. I couldn't believe how beautiful it looked. We just sat on this slope looking at the snow and the sky. Then we built a snowman. I wish I had taken a picture. It probably won't snow for another twenty years.

He pays me. I count forty dollars and smile.

You should get away, I'm thinking, before you start liking it here too much. You'll be working, helping him, and then one day you'll be finished with the yard. And that will be another place you won't be able to come back to.

"Tomorrow I'd like you to paint the front porch. In the meantime, stay out of trouble," he says, like I go looking for it.

Thursday, 12:20 PM

I could find Alicia's house with my eyes closed. Joey and I trekked through the woods to get there a thousand times, if only to have somewhere to go. Sometimes we'd play basketball in her driveway. Sometimes the woods would be flooded so we'd ride our bikes on the busy highway to her house. Cars don't pay attention to bikers or they blow their horns when they're right behind you and you almost jump off your bike. We never told his parents we rode on that highway. They'd go psycho.

One time somebody threw a paper cup out their car window and it hit Joey. He fell off his bike. Then a few minutes later we caught up with the car at a red light. I got off my bike and wrote down the license plate number. The driver rolled down his window and called me a pussy. I shouted at him that he could've killed my friend.

I pull into Alicia's driveway and lean my bike against the rusty basketball post. The net on the hoop has rotted away. Her house has changed over the years. It used to be white, but now it's a faded brown, and there's only one car in the garage instead of two. There also used to be toys scattered in the yard—stuff like a little kid's picnic table with a plastic tea set. Alicia loved playing house. She'd give Joey and me parts to play. I usually got to be the baby. Back then all she wanted was a husband, a baby, and a pink tea set. Joey, Alicia, and I would make a tent from a sheet in her backyard, go inside, and take off our clothes. Then we'd look at each other, point, and laugh.

"Go away, Clay."

I turn around and see Alicia standing on the porch, looking like she did the day her dog, Bandit, died. He used to attend the tea parties too, dressed in an old silk scarf.

"I only want to talk."

"I don't have anything to say."

"I don't care that I wasn't invited to the party," I say. "I needed to work anyway. I just want to know who gave Joey PCP."

Alicia watches me as I'm wilting in the hot sunlight. Across the street a dump truck churns a load of garbage. I glance over—at least my dad's not the driver.

"You're trying to blame us for what you did," she says. "Everybody had a good time without you, and you were mad and jealous and attacked Joey." She goes inside and slams the door hard enough that a beer can falls off the porch railing.

CHAPTER 22

Thursday, 7:15 PM

I'm gently rotating Joey's finger, doing standard range-of-motion exercises, and I'm thinking Alicia could be right about me being mad and jealous that Joey got all the attention. If everybody saw it in me, it must be true.

At least I'm only working a four-hour shift, 7 PM to 11 PM.

I move his thumb around and around and back and forth. Since he's not doing the normal everyday things like dressing or walking, his joints can get stiff and his muscles can deteriorate. He might not be able to play football or ride a bike ever again if he's in a coma for too long. I change to his pointing finger and repeat the exercises. Fingers first, then wrist, next his elbow, and finally his shoulder. The Chanceys saw me in here earlier, but they just continued on to the waiting room.

It's not much, but I feel like I'm helping him. I won't do his neck—I'm not allowed to do that. After I left Alicia's house, I went by Joey's and looked for Champ again. I had to do it. I hadn't been there since Monday and it's already Thursday. He wasn't anywhere around. There wasn't any food or water in his bowls by the shed. I guess I'd run away too if I got left without food and water.

I move to the other side of the bed and start on Joey's right fingers. I talk to him in my mind and I imagine I can watch his responses. See, he doesn't use words. He shows the emotions in his face. I tell him not to be afraid and something in his expression changes.

That's when I start having hope again.

"I think he's in pain," I tell Mildred as I exercise Joey's big toe.

Mildred hangs a new IV bag containing the thick yellow stuff for patients who can't eat. If some gets onto the floor, it glues down your foot.

"I don't think so." She seems certain. "What makes you think he's hurting?"

I move to another toe. "Sometimes I feel like he's watching me. Sometimes his face looks like he's in pain."

"It's your imagination," she says. "We see and hear what we want to, not what is real. I've seen it happen a hundred times when families visit their loved ones. They use anything they can imagine and try to turn it into what they want to see."

She's wrong. It can't be my imagination. I watch the heart monitor. In the few minutes we've been talking, Joey's heart rate has gone from 64 to 99.

I imagine his tube in my throat, the way it presses into his cracked lips and pulls his mouth to one side. Mildred goes out of the room. I finish exercising for Joey.

I stoop and retie his wrist to the side rail. I like to leave him untied when I'm in here to watch him, and anybody can see he's unable to pull any tubes out. I notice how swollen the backs of his hands are. I press his skin with my finger, leaving my print, and his hand weeps tiny drops of fluid like tears. As I stand, the bag of IV fluid knocks me in the head. Maybe it knocks some sense into me because I know Mildred's right. Joey doesn't feel or hear a thing.

Thursday, 9:30 PM

I'm sad and worried about Joey and working hard isn't helping like I thought it would. I've been up and down these floors, mopping and prepping rooms, but I can't escape the image of Joey lying in that bed. I'm mopping a spill on the emergency waiting room floor when a man runs through the double doors. "Help!" he yells. "I need a doctor." I look around for a real doctor. I don't see anybody but a waiting room full of restless patients and the receptionist with a migraine. She jumps up from the desk.

"I'll see what's happening," I tell the receptionist as the man heads outside. I drop the mop, grab a wheelchair, and put on a pair of gloves from a box on the desk. You never know what might be waiting in the parking lot—a stab wound or a hole in one or somebody vomiting. You have to watch out for body fluids like urine and blood. We've had one nurse who caught hepatitis. You never know who might have AIDS. You never know.

Outside, the man's jumping up and down next to a purple Thunderbird in the drive. I push the wheelchair over. In the backseat I see a woman lying flat, her legs spread and bulging in between. I get a little sick.

I swallow. "I'm a med tech," I say in a phony, calm, deep voice. "Everything's fine. Would you tell the receptionist to ask the doctor to step out here for a moment?" I ask the man. "Tell her a baby's being born."

I stick my head into the car. "Can you wait a minute?" I ask the woman, and she starts screaming at me. I guess she can't.

"Don't panic," I say in a calm voice.

I get to be the one who panics.

"Pant," I say.

We can do that together. I've already started.

I get between her legs, brace my knees on the car seat, and stick out my hands like I'm catching a football. "Just think of this as an adventure!" I shout.

She yells, "Go to hell! It's coming! It's coming!"

I see the top of its head streaked with slimy black hair. Nothing's going to slow this baby down. "Push," I tell the woman. She grunts hard. The head slides out and I support it with my hands. I can see a tiny, ugly face. The baby's nostrils flare as it takes a breath. Then the shoulders slide into my hands and I keep supporting the head. The chest is followed by the trunk and legs. Wow. A whole baby. A complete human life.

I cradle the crying creature in my arms. It's blue, and blood and slime cover its body. The umbilical cord's attached. Blood gushes from the woman's vagina and I jump. I watch wide-eyed as her vagina bulges again, and I think, It can't be another baby.

It can't be. Suddenly a purplish glistening afterbirth plops out onto my knee. Fuck. I wonder what to do with that.

My hands shake as I hold the screeching baby. He's a feisty little creature. I glance over my shoulder, looking for the doctor. Or anybody. Somebody save me. Please.

The mother moans. "Is it a girl?" The baby pees straight up into the air and it hits my chin.

I wipe my face on my shoulder. "Boy." I suppose she didn't want to know the sex of the baby beforehand. I place the baby in her arms. The doctor will cut the cord when he gets here.

She starts laughing. "A boy? I hope he likes his four sisters."

I hope she gets a discount from the hospital for having the baby in the car.

"What's your name?" she asks.

"Sorry. I forgot to introduce myself in the excitement. I'm Clay Gardener."

"Clay. That's a good name for a baby born in a driveway." Then the mom's crying and laughing.

A doctor squeezes in beside me. "I'll finish up now, Clay. Good job. Wait for me inside, will you?"

I wonder what took him so long, but thinking back, I realize the whole thing only lasted a couple of minutes. I back out of the car and fall into the wheelchair. I hold my bloody gloved hands in front of me and try to ignore the slimy wetness on my knee.

One minute I'm mopping a floor and the next minute I'm watching a baby explode into the world. I don't know how I can feel so good because of a crying baby who peed on me. All I did was catch him. I wish Joey could've seen this.

I bite my lip. It'll be a great story for him later, anyway.

I take off the gloves, throw them into the trash in the emergency room, and quickly change into clean scrubs. Then I resume mopping the floor. I wonder if I did something wrong. After a few minutes the doctor comes over to me. I stop what I'm doing. He tells me that since this is her fifth child and such a rapid birth, she already had two strikes against her. In many cases like hers the uterus doesn't clamp down when it should, and the mother can bleed to death. He says I did a good job.

Smiling, I hold on to the mop like it's a trophy.

Thursday, 10:05 PM

I'm standing at the entrance to the waiting room trying to eavesdrop on a conversation between Mrs. Chancey and Dr. Sermons. Mrs. Chancey is in her chair by the coffeepot. She's wearing a wrinkled, faded dress and sneakers.

"His vital signs are stable," Dr. Sermons says with a frown. "His chest X-ray was clear this morning."

"But he's not responding," Mrs. Chancey says. She looks over at me and then back at the doctor. She doesn't seem to mind me listening in. "Why isn't he responding?"

Dr. Sermons draws a picture of a brain on a piece of paper and points. "With the subdural hematoma, his brain was pushed to the side by the swelling." She shades in part of the picture. "We removed the clot with surgery, and with the medicine he's on, we're hoping to reduce the pressure inside the brain."

Mrs. Chancey stares at the picture. "But he ought to be responding. I asked the nurse, and she hasn't given Joey any sedation."

"Sometimes it takes time." Dr. Sermons folds the paper in half. "But I am concerned. I've ordered another EEG for in the morning."

Mrs. Chancey looks directly into her eyes. "To see how much brain activity there is?"

"Yes. He's not on any sedation so we'll get a clearer picture."

For a minute neither of them says anything. I have a feeling Dr. Sermons doesn't know what to say. Then she leaves.

"You can come in, Clay," Mrs. Chancey calls weakly.

I go over to her and kneel. I think she's in shock. I turn all the negatives into one big positive. "Things are looking better today. He's totally stabilized and it's really likely he'll wake when the swelling in his brain goes down."

I don't know if it's right or wrong to give her hope, but all I'm doing is presenting the truth from a different angle. I sit beside her. She looks at me and almost smiles. "How's work going?" she asks.

"Busy. I've been running all over the hospital, restocking."

I see her lips tremble, but she's still smiling. "Oh, I saw your sketch with all the tubes labeled. You should make that into an instruction book for families."

I've never thought of that. "You want me to stay the night?"

She runs her hand through the back of her hair. "No, Clay. We'll be here."

"This is all my fault," I blurt suddenly. "I pushed Joey too hard."

It's just Mrs. Chancey and me in the quiet of the waiting room.

She takes a few breaths. "He didn't mean to hurt you. You didn't mean to hurt him." She pulls her handbag into her lap and opens it. She takes out the school's literary magazine. "I needed something to read so I grabbed this from home. I read a story Joey wrote about you. I never knew about it. I read it out loud to Clarence."

I nod. I don't know what I'm supposed to say. People start drifting into the waiting room. A teacher from school comes in, speaks to Mrs. Chancey, and sits next to her. Mr. Chancey walks in with a bag from a fast-food place, and the room smells like french fries. I stand and move over in front of the coffeepot. He sits down. He doesn't speak. He doesn't yell at me. I can stand here and communicate without saying a thing.

CHAPTER 23

Thursday, Late Night

In the middle of the night I hear ringing and I feel around on the coffee table and the floor for the phone. I'm not sure how long ago I staggered home and fell onto the sofa. I was at the hospital very late. I finally find the phone and answer.

"Hi," Michelle says softly, like when she used to call me on the nights we didn't see each other.

I sit straight up. "Are you okay?"

"Will you meet me in the morning at the duck pond? Early? Around seven?"

I think of all the reasons she might want to see me, and all the things I want her to say. I wish I knew how to keep her on the phone. Right now I can make myself believe everything's the way it used to be.

"Okay, but why the duck pond?" I can hardly speak.

"I don't need a reason for every single thing I do." I hear a click, and I start pressing her number to call her back. Don't do this, I'm thinking. You'll regret it. Before I press the last number, I stop and hit the Off button.

It's only been a week since I saw Michelle in the Watering Hole parking lot with that guy. I walked home afterward, sat in front of the window, and drank the rest of the twelve-pack. I watched cars pass.

I stretch out on the couch. I keep thinking about Joey, but somehow I fall asleep. I dream we're on our bikes, and I keep asking, "What are you doing here?" He laughs and shrugs. We head down the highway. I'm completely happy, and then I wake up.

CHAPTER 24

Friday, 7 AM

I lay the bread on the picnic table and look at the muddy, shallow pond. Another week without rain and it'll dry up completely. I sit on the bench and watch the geese on the far side of the pond. Whenever Joey and I come here, we always bring bread for the ducks and the geese and the squirrels.

It wasn't long ago that Michelle and I walked around the pond and fed the ducks. The water was still clear then and it sparkled in the sunlight. We saw a big white bird trying to eat a snake. I don't know what kind of bird it was. The bird sucked the snake almost all the way inside its mouth, but then the snake crawled partway out. Over and over again. Michelle and I held hands and watched, fascinated, and I remember how hard her nails dug into me. She was upset so we left and went to the mall, where I bought her a necklace with part of the money I'd saved for the bike trip. She liked it, and I wanted to make her happy.

I walk over to pond and toss a bread crust. A jogger passes. I figure he's the executive type. Gets up early. Jogs a few miles. Works. Goes home to his family. Takes them to movies. Even plays ball with them. I bet he reads to his kids every night. My dad used to read to me. He'd pick up one of my books and make up what it was saying because he can't read well.

The jogger turns and heads back. He waves to me. I wave back and then I look around and wonder why Michelle's late.

"Are you Clay?" he says when he's about twenty feet away.

"Yeah."

He jogs to where I'm standing and then jogs in place. He pulls a small white box from a pocket in his shorts and hands it to me. "Girl asked me to give this to you."

I open the box and see the gold necklace with the heart I gave Michelle after we were here the last time. Then I still believed we'd be a forever thing. At least a long-term thing. I can't believe she'd do this—have a stranger give me the necklace. "She's gone?" I ask, stupid.

Still jogging in place, he nods.

"Thanks." I turn away. I don't know if I feel more rotten about her returning the necklace or about the fact that she gave it to some stranger to give to me.

I throw the necklace into the pond, and it plops at the edge of the water. He goes over, picks it up, and returns.

"That was really smart," he says. He stops jogging. "It looks like you paid a lot for that necklace."

I'm just standing there thinking that if the worst thing I do from now on is throw away a necklace that I can't get my money back for, I'm lucky. Nobody's acted very smart lately.

"It doesn't matter," I say.

I toss more bread to the geese, hoping he goes away. By now there are at least twenty of them, and they keep moving closer to the bank. Hungry, honking geese surround me. My head's starting to pound. I throw the rest of the bread onto the ground.

The jogger hands me the necklace. "Give this to somebody who really cares about you. She isn't that person." He jogs away.

How could he know that in one minute when I didn't see it for weeks? I walk toward the picnic table holding the empty bread wrapper and necklace.

I stuff the wrapper into the garbage along with the necklace. Then I change my mind. On the way to my bike I pass a car in the parking lot. I stop, open the door, and place the box with the necklace on the seat. In the distance, all the geese are waddling up a parched slope, honking together.

Friday, 4 PM

I ride my bike to Joey's house to search for Champ.

This morning my dad told me he hadn't had time to look for Champ, but he said he would today. I don't believe him.

After I left the duck pond, I went home and slept a few hours. Then I called Chief Baker and told him I'd paint his porch tomorrow when I had a day off. I told him I was heading to Joey's to find Champ.

I'm walking around the backyard calling for Champ when I

hear a car pull into the drive. I trudge to the front yard. Chief Baker's climbing out of his car. I stop cold. "What?" I ask.

Chief Baker frowns. "Joey's mother called. His heart stopped this morning. I knew you were here. I wanted to tell you before you went to the hospital."

"Is he—is he—"

"He was resuscitated. He's critical."

I won't think. I won't listen. My head's spinning. I glance around for Champ and see nothing except the empty yard, the silent highway. I notice how dark the sky is and how one cloud looks like a turkey vulture. Joey knows about birds. His favorite was the bobwhite. We used to hike into the woods and Joey would call to them. My favorite bird is the chicken.

In my mind, I knew this was coming. But my heart feels like it's all a horrible surprise.

"Clay? I'm headed to the hospital. I'll drive you."

I take a breath. It hurts. I didn't think breathing could get harder than it was yesterday. I touch my face and feel the salty stickiness. My shirt is damp with sweat.

"Are you listening to me? Are you working today?" he asks.

I nod and swallow. "At seven."

"I have a golfing friend. It would be a good idea for you to talk with him," he says. "He's a counselor."

I'm not crazy. "Good for you," I struggle to say. "You have a lot of friends. Too bad none of them can feed a cat."

"Actually I stopped seeing them after my wife died."

"So it's okay to ask a loser like me to feed your cat because I won't feel sorry for you."

"This isn't about you feeding my cat."

"Oh, right. It's all about your investigation. Because if you'd seen me as a person, you wouldn't have pretended to be my friend. You act like you have a life, but you don't."

"I saw you as somebody I could trust," Chief Baker says. "You're not to blame for what happened to Joey."

"So who the hell *is* responsible? Never mind. I can't think about that right now. See, I've got another big problem, and I don't know how to handle it."

"What is it?"

It's hard for me to talk.

"If Joey dies, this can't be a coroner's case. Joey cannot have an autopsy. I know they always do one whenever there is a suspicious death. I know you can get it handled differently."

"The coroner has to be notified," Chief Baker says.

"I know he does. Tell him that Joey wanted to be an organ donor. It's on his driver's license. I went with him the day he got it, and we talked. He said he'd want his death to mean something to somebody."

There. I've said it. I look up. The turkey vulture cloud is gone now. Broken up by the wind. Joey's dying is real.

"I can take care of that," Chief Baker says.

CHAPTER 25

Friday, 5:45 PM

I enter ICU. Jan stops me before I get to Joey's room. "You can't go in. Mrs. Chancey is in the chapel and she wants to see you ASAP. She's asked me a half dozen times if I knew when you'd be coming to work." A shiver runs up and down my back. "Mr. Chancey is with Joey."

"How's Joey?" I ask.

"Critical."

In the chapel, Mrs. Chancey's sitting on a pew, hands folded, staring straight ahead. I slide in beside her. We sit shoulder to shoulder facing the dull, sad-looking altar, the fluorescent lights buzzing along with the quiet piped-in organ music.

"I didn't think you were coming. I called your apartment, everywhere."

I look down and shrug. "I came as quick as I could. I didn't even take a shower."

She kind of smiles. "I noticed."

"Any change?"

"He's been the same since this afternoon."

"No chance that it's the medicine?"

"He's not had any sedation for a couple of days now. He hasn't had anything that would interfere with his level of consciousness," she says. "The doctor says there's been a lot of damage . . . irreversible. . . . And that was before his heart stopped."

My breath catches in my chest. I clasp my hands together and listen to the music. The song is "The Old Rugged Cross." I remember it from all the Easter sunrise services I attended with the Chanceys. Joey and I would always sit on the last pew and draw comic strips along the edge of the bulletin.

"I know this is bad to say right now." All I want to do is rest my head against the pew and feel the cold wood against my forehead. "And maybe I'm not the one who should say it, but it would be important to Joey. He wanted to be an organ donor if the time ever came. . . ."

Tears run down her face. "He did?"

"It's on his license," I say.

She touches my back. "I don't want to leave you here alone," she says. "I wanted you to know. But I have to get back. I want to be there in case . . ."

In case his heartbeat starts to slow, in case his blood pressure drops. Just in case. "I won't be alone. I have to get to work," I say. "Ask any nurse to page me. I'll be here."

When I finally make it to the doctors' lounge, I feel weak

and my stomach aches. I shower, get scrubs from a closet, and dress. I check the mirror and see circles under my eyes. I see how pale I look. I put a fake smile on my face and quickly drink a couple of cups of coffee.

I can do this. I can walk down the halls with my assignment sheet. I can be a robot because I've always been good at shutting everything out.

I get paged to the surgical floor. I push everything from my mind except that I have to work. I need this job. The elevator doors shut. I push two, then three. No. Surgical is on four. On the way up, the elevator stops at every floor. People crowd in. They get out. Somebody asks for directions. Everything goes on as normal.

I ride the elevator to the top floor and back down again. I'm shaking when I get to the nurses' station. A man in a black uniform walks up to the desk. "Did somebody here call security?" he says to the nurse.

"Yes," the nurse answers. "I need an escort to the morgue."

I can see his Adam's apple wiggle. Right away I know he's afraid to go down there.

The morgue is the loneliest place in the world. It's isolated, and it's locked. He's got the keys.

"Room four one three. Edward Studdenburg is his name," the nurse says, looking at my name badge. "You'll be going down with Clay."

A creepy feeling washes over me.

She turns to the metal paper-towel holder over the sink and pushes her frizzy red hair away from her face. She's new here, and she's younger than most of the nurses. Her pink scrubs cling to her body like a sausage skin.

"I haven't been trained to do that yet," I say. My words come out slurred and rattled. "I can go with you and help."

She faces me. "It doesn't take a brain surgeon to push a bed," she says. She slams a chart on the desk and keeps looking at me. "What's wrong with you? Have you been drinking?"

The security guard stomps toward the room, his shoes squeaking.

I click on my smile and adjust my attitude. You can do anything or say anything and I won't care because I'm already losing the thing I care about the most in the world.

"No, ma'am," I say. "I'm glad to help out."

"Come on," the security guard says from the hallway. He already has the body out of the room. One hand grips the bed until his knuckles turn white, the other hand pulls the covers over the body. The half-empty bottle of IV fluids is still hanging on the metal pole at the head of the stretcher. I figure that the nurse was busy doing important stuff like looking at herself in the paper-towel holder and forgot to take it down.

I grab the side of the bed. The guard pushes hard and a wheel rolls over the edge of my shoe. I pull my foot out of the way. I rub my toes together. I don't feel blood inside my socks. I don't feel pain. I don't feel anything. I move to the foot of the bed.

The guard mumbles something under his breath. I don't think it's an apology.

The door of the freight elevator opens. Cool air and basement smells drift out. We push the bed inside and stand in separate corners. We don't look at the body.

He hits the elevator button. We drop to the basement. I rub my sweaty hands together. I've left my heart on another floor.

The elevator stops with a bounce and a thud. I push the bed into the dim hallway. Our shadows dance on the wall like specters. Footsteps echo from a side hall. I look behind me. It's cold here. Smells itch my nose. I sneeze, then take a deep breath through my mouth.

We stop at a door, and the guard unlocks it after trying several different keys. He kicks the door and it swings open.

Cool air hits me.

"What do we do now?" I ask. I know I'm not thinking straight. "Don't we have to register the patient or something?"

"I don't know," he answers. "This is my second day on the job."

"Okay," I tell the security guard. "We'll push the bed in and I'll call and ask." I pull the bed over the threshold. The wheel jams in a gap between the floor tiles.

"Can you give me a hand?" I ask.

The security guard squeezes through the door to the foot of the bed. We both pull. The jarring across the threshold shakes the side rail loose. It falls with a clang and the sound echoes off the morgue walls. The body sits halfway up in the bed and then lies back down. I think I hear a moan, but I'm not sure if it's me or the security guard. He reaches for the stick fastened to his belt and raises it, his hand shaking.

"No!" I shout, and grab his arm. "It's only a dead man. He probably has rigor mortis."

The guard pushes away from me and runs faster than somebody on hot coals, and I'm alone.

The dead man grunts.

So I'm not exactly alone. I run to the stretcher and lift the sheet. The body's not wrapped.

"Is my surgery over?" the man says, speech slurred, eyes skinny slits.

"Yes, sir." I start pushing the bed out of the morgue like I'm Superman. "I'll have you back in your room in a few minutes." I look at him. He could pass for dead. "You okay?"

"Fine. Never better." He rolls onto his side and pulls the sheet over his head.

The elevator opens and Sausage Nurse and Mrs. Hunt are standing inside. They don't say anything. I push the bed into the elevator and hold up the wall.

After the patient is safely in his room Mrs. Hunt hands me a cup. "We need a urine specimen," she says, "for a drug test. Charlie will escort you to the bathroom and observe."

Charlie's standing at the nurses' station.

"Afterward, wait in my office. Don't go anywhere." When she turns and walks past me, I get a whiff of the smell of the morgue.

In the bathroom, I piss in the cup. I piss out my pride, too, while Charlie watches. Wipe off the side. Put on the cap. Hand it to Charlie. I don't stand up straight.

"Clay," Charlie says. He starts whispering. "You ever hear that the Chinese symbol for 'crisis' is also the symbol for 'opportunity'?"

I shake my head.

"Well, that's not exactly true, but I believe that crisis can mean opportunity. Say maybe you have slipped up." He looks at the cup. "Maybe this is going to show something that would hurt your chances of working in a hospital or even going to medical school."

"What are you getting at?" I say.

"I'm offering you an opportunity. Pour this out, and I give a specimen."

It's going to be positive. I slipped up once less than a month ago. One fucking time when I was with Michelle in the garden at the funeral home, I tried her pot. I'm sure it will show up. I get to thinking I'd be messing up Charlie's life if anybody found out. I don't want to hurt anybody else. "Thanks," I say. "But I won't do that."

I wash my hands and ask him if he knows anything about PCP.

"It causes hallucinations. We've had a couple of suicides and murder victims brought into the ER to be pronounced over the last year or so. They had either used PCP or been around somebody on it."

I shut off the water. I look in the mirror at him. "You sound like an expert."

He nods. "I learned a few things when I lived in a college dorm. PCP is a hallucinogen like LSD, but it's more dangerous. You never know how somebody will react. But if you try it you may get lucky and only foam at the mouth and feel like you're going to die. The PCP causes dysphoria instead of euphoria." He looks down. "But people keep chasing the high. It's never the same."

"You tried it?"

"Yeah. About a year ago my friends and I rolled up some good weed with PCP."

I swing around. "What?"

"We laced the weed with PCP to give it more of a kick."

I remember hearing that somewhere, but I had forgotten. "You went crazy?" I ask.

"Not really. We smoked awhile, and I felt sick. My chest hurt and I felt like I was falling. I didn't want to jump out the window or anything, but I definitely thought my friends were out to get me."

I get an incident report from a file cabinet at the nurses' station. In the supervisor's office I sit next to the potted plastic plant and fill out the form. I have plenty of time to get the details right.

If Joey were here, he'd have the right words to make them understand.

I won't think about Joey or Michelle. I make an invisible shield around myself. I roll the chair to the desk, pick up the phone, and call Michelle's cell. There's no answer. "It's Clay," I say. "Joey's condition is worse. The doctor doesn't think he'll make it. Just thought you'd want to know. It was you, wasn't it? You gave him marijuana with PCP, didn't you?"

Awhile later Mrs. Hunt appears. She drags her chair from behind her desk and sits. She looks down at the incident report and her bifocals slide to the tip of her nose. After a few minutes of writing, she fixes her eyes on me over the top of her glasses. "Administration has been notified. Since no harm came to the patient and he was never really awake, they feel like what happened isn't an issue. You're not to discuss this with anybody." She takes a deep breath. "We pride ourselves on giving the best possible patient care."

I think about what kind of pride I have. Joey's proud of his grades, his mother, his father. Sometimes he was so proud of stuff I couldn't stand it. "I understand," I say, feeling like I'd rather die than sit here or face anybody in this hospital again. "I forgot to check the patient's identification. It won't happen again."

"Clay, during your training we emphasized the importance of triple-checking the patient's identification before doing anything."

I nod. I cross my legs and untie my shoelace, then tie it again.

"Do you have anything else you want to say?"

My hands are wet with cold sweat. I clear my throat. "How is the patient?"

The tips of her ears turn red. "He's resting comfortably. The first time you asked me for a job, I laughed. You had a lot of nerve, expecting to be hired without any training. You kept coming back and checking for an opening. I saw hope. You had the kind of motivation I like seeing in an employee so I took a leap of faith. I've heard good things about you, Clay." She takes a deep breath. "Just today I received a letter from a boy who'd been in the emergency room who seems to think you're special. I've never received a letter of thanks from a child before."

The kid who wanted yellow stitches.

"And I have a letter of commendation from an emergency room physician. I understand you delivered a baby the other night." She looks down. "I don't expect anyone to be perfect. We all make mistakes. I've made my share." She looks at the incident report. "Now for the bad part. I'm sorry, but I'm asking for your resignation effective immediately."

CHAPTER 26

Friday, 9:50 PM

One Saturday Joey and I went to the Wolf Theater downtown. The special admission price was a dollar plus six cans of vegetables for the homeless shelter. We watched a Western about this man who was going to be shot because he'd accidentally killed a man. He stood before the firing squad, said he was sorry to the victim's family, and faced his executioners, refusing to be blindfolded. I didn't see what happened next because I shut my eyes, but I heard the gunshots.

I have to make sure the patient's okay. I head down the hall, stop outside the room, and build up my courage. What if the man is permanently scarred from what happened, or what if I'd left him in the morgue? Say he has a wife and a little kid and that little kid had to grow up without a dad. Maybe without a mom, too, because she's so upset she can't cope. The kid grows up poor and scared and made fun of and not ever understanding what happened, only that a small mistake messed up a lot of lives.

But you didn't hurt the patient.

You have to see for yourself so you know.

I step into the room. Mrs. Hunt would kill me if she knew I was doing this.

A woman stands by the bedside feeding the patient ice chips. I go over to them and hang on to the curtain. The sound of something crashing to the floor in the hall breaks the silence in the room.

I think I know how the man felt looking at all those guns pointed at him.

"Hello," the woman says. I nod.

"How are you?" I ask the man.

"Fine."

"Can I get you anything?"

He shakes his head and smiles.

I turn and walk away. This sucks in a lot of ways. I can't even say I'm sorry.

Friday, 10:01 PM

In the waiting room of the ICU, Mr. and Mrs. Chancey look like they've been crying. I go over and kneel between them. "What's going on?" I ask, looking at Mr. Chancey.

Mr. Chancey wipes his face with a snotty handkerchief. "The doctor says Joey has no brain activity on his EEG. They need more tests to confirm. And another opinion."

Trembling, I close my eyes. "It isn't fair," I say. "It just isn't fair."

"We won't know until tomorrow," Mr. Chancey says.

Mrs. Chancey takes my head between her hands and kisses my forehead. "Darcy, your father, and you have been so good to us and to Joey." I feel her tears on my face. They feel the same as mine.

"You don't hate me?"

"No," they say together. Mr. Chancey says he walked into the room when I was bathing Joey and singing. He says it about tore him apart. He says he's sorry about burning my clothes. He doesn't know what came over him.

Friday, 10:07 PM

Charlie sits at the nurses' station inside the unit. I glance into Joey's room. His heart is still beating, his chest rising and falling, every breath of air forced into his lungs.

"Hey, Clay, I'm sorry about everything," Charlie says. "Anyway, I wanted to tell you, it stinks. The whole thing stinks."

I force a smile. "A cup of piss usually does," I say. I keep my eyes on Joey's room. I try to act normal.

"Mrs. Hunt threw it out," Charlie says.

"What?"

"That's all I'm saying."

Friday, 10:10 PM

I slip into Joey's room, close the door, and take his hand. For a few minutes I stand by his bedside. Then I fix his covers, put artificial tears into his eyes, and turn the TV to the cartoon channel. "I can't stay," I say. "Your father and mother will want to spend as much time as they can alone with you. But it's going to be okay. Everything's going to be okay."

I know it is, I imagine Joey saying. I wish I could talk to them. You know. Say goodbye.

I never say goodbye. "We can't change things, can we? Not this time. Can't undo the mistakes."

After we watched that movie at the Wolf Theater, Joey and I went back to the shed. We tried to figure out a better ending for the movie—one in which the man wouldn't be executed. But we had to change what happened at the beginning to make it end right.

"Clay, you need to leave," Charlie says from the doorway. "Joey's going to have more tests, and you have an outside call. I answered the call and put it on hold for you."

I get a lump in my throat. "I need a favor. Joey's parents will want to stay with him. If there's time, will you give him a quick bath first?" So he doesn't smell.

Charlie nods. "Whatever you want."

I can't stand pity. My eyes sting. I'm trembling inside but I don't let him see.

I think, I could've gotten help for Joey before it was too late.

CHAPTER 27

Friday, 10:19 PM

I pick up the phone in the conference room of the unit, hoping no one will walk in. I shouldn't even be here. I don't work here anymore. "You called, Clay," Michelle says. Her voice is slurred. "Whaddya want?"

"You gave Joey marijuana laced with PCP," I say.

"And embalming fluid," she murmurs. "Hold on. I need to lie down."

I don't move. I clutch the phone. "What?"

"To make it better. I know, you hate me. I'm everything you think I am."

"Why are you telling me this? I won't keep anything secret."

"It doesn't matter now," she says. "Please don't say anything about the embalming fluid, though. I don't want my family to get in trouble."

I hear people talking outside the door. "Are you all right?" I ask quickly.

"I didn't mean for any of this to happen."

I can barely understand her. "Where are you?"

She yawns. "It's late. I'm so tired."

"You were at the party in the woods, weren't you?"

Her voice trembles. "I told Joey I liked him a lot. He told me to leave him alone."

Michelle's crying as she tells me the story. Joey was so drunk he could barely stand up. Alicia and Wade took him back to the shed. Michelle followed. She wanted Joey and her to hook up. They smoked. They drank more. Soon Joey was totally wasted. They thought he'd be all right. They thought he was just bombed. Alicia and Wade had sex and went back to the party. I guess that was the condom I saw in the garbage can. Michelle came on to Joey. He got even crazier. He called Michelle the devil. He threw bottles. He kicked over the table. She was afraid of him. She ran through the woods to the party. She told Wade and Alicia. They were scared to return to the shed. They knew they could get into trouble. They decided to go home and not say anything. Alicia went nuts with concern. She made Wade stop at a gas station on the way home. She called 911 from a pay phone.

"Now you can be happy. You know everything and I'm a bitch and I'm going to be out of your life," Michelle says.

"You have a cell phone. You could've called for help. You saw how fucked up he was."

"I know. Don't worry."

An internal alarm goes off. "Did you take something?"

"Thirty pills. It's too late for you to do anything even if you wanted to."

I close my eyes. "Where are you?"

"Somewhere I can't fuck up anybody anymore." Her voice is heavy and slow now.

"Don't do this, Michelle," I say, hoping she's just being dramatic, that she's lying about the pills. There's no answer. "Michelle?"

My legs get weak and shaky. I hear silence.

"Michelle! You have no right to do this!"

She doesn't answer.

I grab the phone book from the shelf, fumble through the pages, and find the number of the funeral home. I call and a man answers. I ask for Michelle.

"She's asleep," he answers gruffly.

My heart's beating wildly. I try to remain calm. "My name is Clay Gardener. I just talked to Michelle. I think she's trying to kill herself."

"You're the son of a bitch who's been bothering Michelle!" he yells. "You could get into a lot of trouble."

"Who's calling?" a woman says in the background.

"It's a prank call," he tells her. "I could have you fired," he tells me. "I know you're calling from the hospital."

"Listen to me," I say. "I'm sorry to bother you, but I think Michelle's taken an overdose. She called me upset. She needs help immediately."

"And why would she do that?"

"Our friend is dying," I say. "And she did some stuff."

There's a long pause. "Go check Michelle!" I hear him finally yell to the woman. Then he says to me, "And if you're playing a sick joke on us, you're going to wish you were the one dead."

How can anybody in the business of helping grieving people not give a rat's ass about his own daughter?

"You fucking bastard," I say. "You're her dad. You're supposed to love her!"

"I didn't mean it the way it sounded. I don't know what I'm saying. Is this a prank call? God, I hope it is a prank! You're probably getting off by hearing all this." He sounds panicky now.

I hear Michelle's mother screaming for him to hang up and call an ambulance. I hang up. I run out of the conference room, through the doors of the ICU, and into the hall. I weave past Chief Baker and a group of people.

He grabs my arm. "What's happening?" Alicia and Wade stand a few feet away.

"I think Michelle took an overdose," I say. "I called her parents. They called an ambulance."

"You're not going to the emergency room," he says. "Don't get involved in it."

"I'm not. I need air. I'm going to the roof."

He releases my arm. "I'll find out what's going on." He heads for the elevator.

I turn toward Alicia and Wade. "You liars. You knew all the time," I say. "And Michelle's just tried to kill herself." I walk away. Down the hall, into the exit. Up a flight of stairs. Up another. Crying. Moaning. Voices echo. Brain death. Suspicion. Redemption. Stupidity. The sounds of the hospital replay: The words of the patient who wasn't dead, the endless buzz of the heart monitor of the girl in the accident, the crying of a newborn, and Joey going crazy. The noises get louder and louder. I grab my head with my hands before it explodes.

I lunge through the door and step into the mist that shrouds the roof. It is shockingly cold after the heat of this week. I stumble to the roof's edge and lean over the rusty rail. My head keeps spinning. I wipe my mouth. My hand carries Joey's smell.

My chest tightens like it has a strap around it, or maybe it's just too full to hold any more pain. I inspect the metal railing. I think about the nurse.

Her ghost haunts this roof. She killed a patient by giving him the wrong dose of a drug. The nurse came up here and jumped. Landed on the loading dock. Did she feel the hot tar on her face before she died? I wonder. Did she find redemption?

I've always tried. I never fit in. I was never good enough, never smart enough. Tonight I could've caused a patient to die if he hadn't woken up at the right time. I couldn't take care of my best friend. I couldn't even stop Michelle from suicide. I probably pushed her to it. She wasn't there for me, so I made sure not to be there for her.

I look down. The dead street winds around the hospital and side roads branch off it like the arteries of a heart. I bet if somebody looked at my heart right now all they'd see would be a quivering mass of scars. I push back the hair hanging in my eyes and plaster the strands to my forehead with spit and tears.

Finally an ambulance arrives, sirens going full blast. I watch as the EMTs open the back doors and slide out the gurney. I see a car pull up and two people climb out. I'm pretty sure they're Michelle's parents. They chase the gurney. I can see a face full of anguish. A man carrying a pocketbook.

She's got a chance, I want to yell. In a moment they'll be

cutting off her shirt, starting IVs, putting a tube into her to help her breathe, putting another one in to pump her stomach. Your daughter's got a chance. They'll give everything they've got to save her.

I've seen what I came here for. Now for the rest. I'm going to miss this place.

I take my CPR card out of my wallet and my name badge from my uniform. I remove the golden heart from my collar, the one I got for being employee of the month. I run my fingers over them and then raise my hand into the air and throw everything as far away as I can. They scatter and fall in different directions. The plastic name badge hangs suspended for half a heartbeat. It falls. A sudden gust of wind blows it away.

I picture Joey riding his bike fast down the highway, laughing and calling to me to hurry and catch up. I picture us on the cross-country trip, him in front, shielding me from the wind.

I'm going to miss him.

I smile for a moment. We had some good times, Joey and me. It hurts to remember the good.

I hear the squeak of the door to the stairs. I turn and see Wade and Alicia coming toward me. Wade's limping. His knee must be bothering him. He puts his arm across my shoulders. "We thought Joey was safe when we left him," Wade says, his voice full of pain.

"We believed you hurt Joey," Alicia says. "We didn't know about the PCP. I'm sorry."

"Michelle said you probably went psycho with jealousy, and she said if we told anybody about the pot, we'd all be in trouble since we were there too. We took one hit from a joint and that was all. It didn't taste right. Believe it or not, we were only trying to keep you out of all this. We figured he'd get well and everything would be forgotten." Wade starts crying.

I saw him cry when he played his final football game. It was a big game with only seconds left. The score was tied 7 to 7. Wade faded back and passed the ball to Joey. Joey made the touchdown. The game was over. We went crazy. I saw Wade withering and crying on the ground. He'd been sacked by the other team. Minutes later he was carried off the field on a stretcher with a knee injury.

He's sobbing harder than he did the night he injured his knee. Alicia's trying to hold him, and she's crying too.

We made the regional playoffs. But we didn't win any more games. Not without Wade.

"Joey was our friend, and we loved him," Alicia says.

The three of us stand along the railing, staring into the mist. I don't know how much time has passed when I hear footsteps.

"Clay?"

I turn and see Chief Baker heading toward us. He glances at Wade and Alicia and then turns to me. "I thought you should know," he says. "You saved her life."

CHAPTER 28

Friday, 11:59 PM

As I open the door of my apartment, the storm begins. Thunder booms and lightning streaks through the gray of the night. The rain comes after all these weeks. Before I left the hospital, I asked Chief Baker if he'd talked to the coroner and Mrs. Hunt. He had. He told me Michelle had had her stomach pumped, had been admitted and placed on suicide watch. He told me to go home.

The lights are off and I can see my dad asleep on the sofa.

Rain pounds the roof. I turn on the kitchen light but it pops and dies. I think about how Joey and I would sit in the shed on stormy nights and tell each other horror stories. We loved being scared to death. In the dark, I cry silently and listen to the rain. I don't hear anything else—not even my dad snoring. I go over to the couch and shake him. He's soft and hairy and smells like a dog.

He *is* a dog. Champ lifts his head, and I shout out, "Champ!" I stroke him, talk dog-talk in a choked-up voice, and sit. He rests his head in my lap.

I wait. This is the best I can do for now. The phone's on the coffee table where I can get to it in case there's a call. Sometime tonight or in the morning two doctors will examine Joey, discuss his case, and look at all the tests to determine if he's suffered brain death. They'll make a decision. I swallow hard. I know the ending this time.

Joey will remain on life support—but at this point it's really organ support. Joey's doctor, along with a chaplain and someone from the organ procurement agency, will walk to the waiting room. The Chanceys will know it's not good. They'll go to a conference room. In my mind's eye I can picture them walking and these are the most painful steps they'll ever take. I know what's next. The doctor will speak to Joey's parents. His voice will be gentle when he says he's sorry, that Joey's brain has ceased to function even though his heart beats because of the machines. He'll explain what brain death is, that Joey's been examined by two doctors, has had tests, and that there's no chance of recovery. He'll say Joey is legally dead. The doctor's eyes will be teary.

He'll ask if they want Joey to give the gift of life. This is what Joey would want. It's on his driver's license.

I sob silently with my face in Champ's hair.

In a few days somebody from the admissions committee at Duke will make a call to another applicant from the wait list and say there's an opening. That person will wonder why. He'll celebrate.

My dad comes into the living room yawning. "I thought I heard you," he says, and nods toward Champ. "I broke him out of jail today."

I wipe my face. "Jail?"

"He was in the dog pound. We'll take him home tomorrow or the next day."

Dad sits and places his arm on the back of the couch.

"Thanks. But that's not like you," I say roughly, suddenly feeling angry. "I'm surprised you bothered."

He sits up as straight as the sagging sofa allows. "What do you mean, Clay?"

"I mean you're never around." I let out a sob, thinking about my dad asleep on the couch, Joey in his hospital bed, Champ in a concrete cell at the pound. "You never help me. I don't know what to do." I try to stop my tears from falling. I try to press down my hurt and rage and sadness and swallow it all whole. I don't expect him to respond. A big part of me wants to get up and walk away before he says something dumb, like everything will turn out all right, or that I should just wait and let things settle down.

After a moment of silence he sighs and rests a hand on my shoulder. "You're just like me, only a lot smarter. Always wanting something beyond your reach. I wanted you to grow up knowing how to take care of yourself." His hand drops to my back and he starts scratching it the way he used to when I was little. "That way you'd learn how to get what you wanted."

"But I don't know how. Nothing is how I want it, Dad. Everything is fucked up. Don't you see that?"

"That's not true. I'm proud of what you've accomplished."

"Yeah, right," I say.

"And your mom would be too."

He goes on to tell me how he was always keeping tabs on me. He knew when I'd sneak off to Joey's house—he always asked Mr. Chancey to call and let him know if I was spending the night there. He called the hospital a bunch over the past couple of days, to find out Joey's status and to check if I was working, if I was okay. He even talked to Mrs. Hunt.

I try to laugh. "I bet she had a lot to say." I wonder if she told him I was fired.

"She said you were one of the best employees she's ever worked with," he says.

We sit in silence for a little while, his hand scratching my back. In just a few moments we've exchanged more words than we have all year.

"You know," he says finally, "your mother wanted you so much. She told me every day until the day you were born. You made her really happy."

Saturday, 8:05 AM

"Wake up, Clay," my dad says.

My head's resting against his shoulder. Champ's head is in my lap. I never figured a dog and my dad would help me make it through the worst night of my life.

Late last night I got a call from Chief Baker. He told me

Michelle was going to be okay. The police went to her house and found a note saying she'd gotten the marijuana laced with PCP at her boarding school in New Hampshire. Turns out it was a school for troubled teens. Michelle's parents sent her there after they found out she was drinking and having sex in junior high. That's where she learned about adding embalming fluid. Chief Baker said embalming fluid supposedly enhances the effects of PCP. He also said that PCP is sometimes called embalming fluid, but they are not the same.

"Today's your eighteenth birthday," Dad says. I sit up. I'm so tired.

"Don't say happy," I say.

"I won't. Mrs. Chancey called. She asked us to come."

"Is it over?"

"All she said was they needed us. That's what's important right now."

I shower and dress in jeans and a shirt. As I'm combing my hair, I think about Joey's valedictorian speech. Instead of a traditional speech, he called out names of the members of our class one by one and said something special about each person. He could always make other people feel extraordinary. I close my eyes. I remember Joey lifting his arm and waving. I remember the thrill, the pride that ran through me. We had finally made it, Joey and me. I remember his closing words that night. "Thank you. Goodbye for now. Go forth and save the world." I stand up straight and puff out my chest like I'm brave and strong and not afraid to move forward. I don't know who I'm being strong for. Joey? My dad? Myself?

I pull my dad's raggedy truck onto the road. He's in the passenger seat. We've left Champ sleeping on the couch. My bike's in the back. When today is over, I'm going to ride away. Hard and fast. But I won't go far, not yet—maybe just to the dead end past Joey's house, or the creek. Somewhere he would have known to look. I press on the gas and I imagine that I'm in a spaceship, floating endlessly in space with no way to go home again.

CHAPTER 29

Saturday, 8:30 AM

We meet the Chanceys in the hall outside the ICU. The looks on their faces tell me that Joey was pronounced brain-dead. We all hug each other. I'm kind of surprised Dad and I the only ones with them.

"Come on," my dad says. "Let's go down to the cafeteria. We can talk and have coffee and then when you're ready I'll drive you home. I'll help you with the arrangements."

They nod. My dad's taking care of them. He's doing what I never thought he'd be able to do.

"I would like to see Joey," I say.

"You can go in," Mr. Chancey says. "They're almost ready for him in the operating room."

"We've said goodbye," Mrs. Chancey whispers, breaking down into sobs.

I watch as my dad leads them away.

My legs are as heavy as anchors as I head into the ICU. I step inside Joey's room and creep up to the hospital bed. The room is dim and the breathing machine hums like ocean waves against the shore. Our last stop on the bicycle trip was going to be the Pacific. I can picture us standing on a cliff watching the waves rush to the shore.

I touch Joey's arm and my hand soaks up the clammy coolness of his skin. I hear the beating of his heart on the monitor and watch the white dot move up and down.

"Hey, Joey." I run my hand along his arm. "I know you probably can't hear me, but just in case, I want to tell you, we'll be fine. Champ, your parents. Me too."

My eyes sting. "Champ was with me this morning. I think he really misses you."

A nurse I don't recognize walks into the room. She checks the machines, glances at Joey, then me. "Are you his brother?" She doesn't wait for an answer. "You favor him a lot."

I think of the bottle we spit in long ago. How we shook it up. How we put it on a shelf. I wonder where that bottle is now.

"His hair . . . do you want a lock?"

I nod. She hands me her bandage scissors. I grasp a lock of his limp, oily hair, and I clip.

The nurse walks out of the room.

I smile. "What am I going to do with your hair? It'll be kind of creepy when I find it in a box years from now, uh?" I feel tears run down my cheeks.

"I never told you that was a great speech you gave at graduation, by the way. I bet that was the best speech ever given by the class valedictorian. You did good. You didn't even sound scared."

I look out the window, at the little cars below, the dull green of the trees. Everything looks artificial. My real life has funneled down to this instant, and my whole body aches with the realization that it's going to be over within minutes.

I can't say any more. I want to tell him not to be scared now, that he's going somewhere better, but the connection between my brain and my mouth is broken. All I can do is watch my best friend breathe evenly with the machine. Suddenly I see how peaceful he looks, like he's ready for whatever comes next.

Two operating room technicians arrive. They disconnect some of the wires and roll the bed out into the hall. I walk all the way to the operating room with Joey. I go as far as I can, and then I release his hand.

EPILOGUE

Nine Months Later
Miles Biked: 1294.5

I'm on a highway in Texas. According to Joey's map, it's only six more miles to Endurance. I take a chocolate bar from the basket and eat it to get a final burst of energy. I keep my eyes on the road because I never know when there'll be a pothole to knock me on my ass.

For a while, I was broken—it was like half of me had been buried. I cried myself to sleep a lot of nights. I've gone to counseling. I've hung out with Chief Baker. He told me the cause of Joey's death was trauma after drug inhalation. It was ruled accidental. He's asked if I want to go into law enforcement. My answer has always been the same. "I want to be a doctor." Some things never change.

I won't ever forget how it was with Joey. Sometimes I dream

about him talking about our trip, making plans, giving me tips. In a way, he's biking with me to the Pacific Ocean. Almost everything I have with me, he touched a hundred times. He was right when he said to take only what you need. His touring bike—the one I'm riding—and gear weighed forty pounds exactly when I left the Chanceys' house twenty-five days ago. My dad and Chief Baker were there with Joey's parents. So were Darcy and Vic. They're married now. Who would have thought?

Everybody stood on the edge of the front yard—Champ, too—and waved and cheered. It was a big send-off. I did not dip my rear tire in the Atlantic Ocean like Joey and I planned. Instead I dipped it in the creek in the woods.

Every few days, I call or e-mail Wade—aka FelixCat. He's in Alaska blogging my progress cross-country, charting my course on a map so the people at home can see. Alicia helps. They want me to visit. I have the time—I don't need to be back until September, when classes start at the community college where I'll be a sophomore. Going to class and working at the nursing home have helped me.

I bite my lip to stop the quivering. I've called Michelle's father three times. He said she was doing fine at college. He didn't say where and I didn't ask. I'll remember her forever, and sometimes I get sad knowing that the person I loved never existed.

The sun's blistering hot, but the roads in Texas are better than in Louisiana. Not to dis Louisiana. I met some of the politest drivers in the world there. They'd honk their horns and wave. I think about Mississippi. It rained a lot, and I was glad Joey wrote "rain gear" on the supply list. Mostly I remember the man who had a heart attack at the wheel of his car and crashed.

I stopped and did CPR. Nobody but Joey would've thought about including a face mask with a one-way valve in the first-aid kit. When the ambulance arrived I got back onto my bike and kept going. Sometimes I get the feeling Joey is on a bike behind me. Sometimes when I pedal uphill, I feel he's in front shielding me from the wind.

I pull out a bottle of water from the basket and drink. I'm certain I've consumed an ocean of water since I left.

I know this cross-country trip won't change what is. But I need to do it. Because it's always been hard for me to show I loved anybody and harder for them to love me back.

The sugar fix takes hold. I'm pedaling, sweating, panting, but I can do this. I feel lighter than ever. It's like my tires have left the highway and I'm flying. I see the WELCOME sign in the distance, and I know Endurance is only spitting distance away.

AUTHOR'S NOTE

Phencyclidine, or PCP, is an unpredictable drug with psychological effects. Thousands of people are brought to emergency rooms each year after using PCP and placed on suicide watch or restrained because they are violent. If a friend or loved one becomes violent, unconscious, or suicidal, starts trembling, acts confused, or has a seizure after using any drug, call 911. If you want to know more about PCP and other drugs, see below.

NIDA
National Institute on Drug Abuse
National Institutes of Health
6001 Executive Boulevard, Room 5213
Bethesda, MD 20892-9561
www.drugabuse.gov/infofacts/pcp.html

Partnership for a Drug-Free America
405 Lexington Avenue, Suite 1601
New York, NY 10174
www.drugfree.org/intervention

Substance Abuse & Mental Health Services Administration
U.S. Department of Health and Human Services
1 Choke Cherry Road
Rockville, MD 20857
http://findtreatment.samhsa.gov/
1-800-662-HELP

Ellwood, William N, PhD. " 'Fry:' A Study of Adolescents' Use of Embalming Fluid with Marijuana and Tobacco." Texas Commission on Alcohol and Drug Abuse, 909 West 45th Street, Austin, Texas 78758; www.dshs.state.tx.us/sa/research/populations/fry.pdf.

ACKNOWLEDGMENTS

Thanks to Ralph Neighbor, MD; Sharyn Brekhus, MD; Jean Watson; and Rex Gardner, RT, for providing expert medical opinions; and John Wood and Jason Mitchell, for sharing their knowledge of police procedures. Any errors are the fault of the author. I owe an enormous debt of gratitude to Cathy Atkins and A. M. Jenkins, who provided help and support from the beginning. Thanks also to Judy Gregerson, Gail Martini, Martha Moore, Diane Shore, Linda Joy Singleton, Jessica Swaim, Laura Wiess, Verla Kay's blue board, and Barbara Perris. Special thanks go to my agent and friend, Steven Chudney, who always believed in the manuscript, and to Joe Cooper, editor extraordinaire. Last but not least, thanks to Claudia Gabel for her insight and support, and to all the folks at Delacorte Press who played a role.

ABOUT THE AUTHOR

As a teenager, S. A. Harazin worked as a nursing assistant at a small hospital, where she did just about everything. She then attended nursing school at Samford University in Birmingham, Alabama. After completing nursing school, she worked in the ICU, the CCU, the ER, and the recovery room at various hospitals. She lives in Georgia with her husband, Tom, and their children, Patrick, Katie, and Andrew.